# "What are you doing here?"

"Now, now. Is that any way to greet the man you're dating?"

Molly's reflexes shot to life and she whispered, "Get in here," before snatching the front of his T-shirt and yanking him inside.

The problem came when she didn't sidestep quickly enough and the solid, muscular wall of Kaleb's chest crashed into her, forcing him to wrap an arm around her to steady them both. The cotton of his shirt was soft and worn under her fingers, and when she took a steadying breath, she inhaled the lemon-and-cedar scent of his soap.

He wiggled his eyebrows and said, "This greeting's more like it."

"Huh?" His hand slid lower until it cupped the rounding curve just below her waistband, and her palms instinctively moved up over his pecs toward his wide shoulders.

"I said, this greeting is more like one I would expect from my girlfriend."

\* \* \*

**AMERICAN HEROES:**
**They're coming home—and finding love!**

P9-BBT-645

Dear Reader,

I have a close friend who was diagnosed with type 1 diabetes as a juvenile. When I first met her, I was in college and had heard of the condition before, but hadn't actually known anyone who dealt with it on a daily basis. While I was fascinated with the concept of finger pricks and blood sugar readings and insulin shots, I never fully processed the impact it had on a person's life until I began writing *A Proposal for the Officer*.

In this book, air force captain Molly Markham doesn't get diagnosed as a type 1 diabetic until she's an adult, which throws her military career as a pilot and her lifestyle completely off course. Meeting know-it-all billionaire Kaleb Chatterson doesn't help things go any smoother.

Doing the research for this book, I realized how much this condition can take a toll on one's physical and mental health. While I understand that each person's journey with diabetes is different, I hope that my portrayal of it in this book is reflected accurately. Any mistakes I made in conveying my research are mine alone.

For more information on my other books in the Sugar Falls, Idaho series, visit my website at christyjeffries.com, or chat with me on Twitter, @ChristyJeffries. You can also find me on Facebook, Facebook.com/authorchristyjeffries, and Instagram, Instagram.com/christy_jeffries. I'd love to hear from you!

Enjoy,

*Christy Jeffries*

# A Proposal for the Officer

*Christy Jeffries*

**HARLEQUIN® SPECIAL EDITION**

Recycling programs
for this product may
not exist in your area.

ISBN-13: 978-1-335-46562-7

A Proposal for the Officer

Copyright © 2018 by Christy Jeffries

**Printed in U.S.A.**

**Christy Jeffries** graduated from the University of California, Irvine, with a degree in criminology, and received her Juris Doctor from California Western School of Law. But drafting court documents and working in law enforcement was merely an apprenticeship for her current career in the dynamic field of mommyhood and romance writing. She lives in Southern California with her patient husband, two energetic sons and one sassy grandmother. Follow her online at christyjeffries.com.

### Books by Christy Jeffries

### Harlequin Special Edition

#### *Sugar Falls, Idaho*

*A Family Under the Stars*
*The Makeover Prescription*
*The Matchmaking Twins*
*From Dare to Due Date*
*Waking Up Wed*
*A Marine for His Mom*

Visit the Author Profile page at Harlequin.com.

To Brooklyn Bender, one of my best friends and a wealth of knowledge when it comes to Boston, *Top Gun*, hockey, New Kids On The Block and type 1 diabetes. Thank you for answering my endless questions. You're never stingy when it comes to giving me feedback, constructive or otherwise. IAJS.

# Chapter One

Leaning against a stack of cases of bottled water, Captain Molly Markham put a hand to her head as nausea overwhelmed her. Closing her eyes for a second, she debated whether or not she was at risk of passing out right there in the middle of Duncan's Market. She grabbed a liter of water off the shelf, unscrewed the cap and took a big swig. Her mouth was dry and suddenly her body felt weighted down.

*Oh, no. It was happening again.*

She'd sworn to the Bureau of Personnel reviewing her medical board that she could keep these episodes under control, but apparently they'd been right to doubt her.

Molly heaved herself off the tower of water and put one foot in front of the other, needing to get as far away from the curious glances of the shoppers who were sure to know her sister, Maxine, and would be only too eager to ask Maxine about her little sister's "incident" out in public.

She needed space and she needed to think. Maybe somewhere to lie down, too. Like her rental car. She grabbed another bottle and made it to the exit before she realized she'd left her purse back in the grocery basket. Damn. She also hadn't paid for the water.

When she did a one-eighty, her hip banged into a giant bag of ice. Or was it a bag of limes? A man dropped both as he reached out a hand to steady her.

That was gonna leave a bruise. The ice, not the guy's hand. His grip was actually gentle and balanced her. His black framed glasses made him look smart, serious. Maybe he was a doctor. Or a reporter.

He kind of had a Clark Kent vibe going for him. At least from the neck up. She took in his blue hooded sweatshirt and checkered canvas sneakers. Maybe *The Daily Planet* had sent him to do an undercover exposé of a nearby skate park.

"Are you okay?" He enunciated like a record player on a low speed. Or was it her hearing that was set to slow motion? It felt like someone had replaced her brain with hot, heavy sand. She licked her lips.

"Of course I'm okay. At least, I think I am." Molly lowered her own voice when she noticed the cashier staring in their direction. "By any chance, do you know how many carbs are in a fruit smoothie?"

His straight white teeth were visible beneath his smirk. "Probably a lot more than the ones in that peach muffin you gobbled down back by the juice bar thirty minutes ago."

"Oh, crap." It was good thing he was holding on to

her arm because trying to mentally calculate how much sugar she'd recently ingested made her want to sink to her knees. "The teenager behind the counter said they were organic."

"You mean the kid who also told you the baked goods on display were half price since they'd been sitting out since this morning and it was now late afternoon?"

Wait. How did this guy know what she'd talked about with the store employee? "Have you been following me?"

"No. I was sitting at that wrought iron table in the back of the store, trying to answer some work emails, but a bunch of clanging drew my attention to the display of soup cans at the end of an aisle. You were stocking up on the minestrone as though a blizzard had just been predicted." He tapped something on his watch and showed her the sunshine icon on the tiny display screen. "It hasn't, by the way. But then I saw you again when you were slouching against your shopping cart in the freezer section where you almost took out a display of ice-cream cones. Are you going to be sick or something?"

She didn't feel any less confused after that description of her sluggish attempts to make her way through the store. Or dizzy. "I don't think so."

"Come on," he said, and moved his hand to the small of her back. "There's a bench right outside and you can sit down."

"I need my purse," she said. *You also needed to use the restroom*, her bladder said.

"Where is it?" he asked.

The guy looked familiar, but his non-military-regulation hairstyle eliminated him as someone she'd served with. Molly had only been in Sugar Falls a few hours, yet her gut told her this man wasn't a local, either. Of course, she'd also been pretty convinced that anything with fruit in it was healthy so perhaps she shouldn't be so quick to listen to her instincts.

*Who are you?* she wanted to know. But she didn't exactly have time for formal introductions. Instead, she replied, "Back by the bottled water."

"Okay, stay here," he ordered as he sprinted away. Yeah, right. Molly wasn't about to stand around and wait. She weaved toward the parking lot, her only plan to get to the safe privacy of her rental car.

Her feet had barely hit the pavement when the Good Samaritan jogged up beside her, her very feminine tote bag swinging from his very masculine shoulder. "Should I call someone?"

"No," Molly said, her eyelids widening in frustration despite the fact that she wanted to close them and take a nap. "I don't want anyone to know."

"To know what?"

She clamped her teeth together, wishing she would've done so sooner to keep those telling words from slipping out.

"Never mind." She pulled the key fob out of her pocket. "The little white Toyota over there is mine."

"I seriously doubt you should be driving right now."

"I've got it," she ground out, despite the fact that she was practically leaning against him as he steered her toward the passenger side of her rental car. She collapsed down on the seat as soon as he got the door open, then she began digging in her purse.

Another wave of nausea tumbled through her as she unzipped a small black case. Ignoring the man's raised brows, she turned on the little machine, inserted a fresh test strip and pricked her finger. It took all of her focus to press the droplet of blood to the litmus paper. There was a series of beeps before the dinging alarm signaled that her glucose level was way too high. Stupid smoothie. And muffin. She should've known better. And she would have, if she hadn't been so starving after dropping her nephew off at baseball practice. She'd thought she'd been so smart, swinging by the market to pick up real groceries instead of grabbing a Snickers at the Little League snack bar while she waited.

It seemed to take hours for her to dial the correct dose on her insulin pen.

"What are you doing?" The panic in his voice probably matched the horror in his eyes. But Molly didn't have the energy to explain. She pulled up the hem of her shirt, not caring that she was exposing herself to the poor man. She could administer the shot in her arms or thighs, but the doctor said it would get into her system a lot quicker if she injected it into her stomach. She didn't even feel the sting of the needle and could only hope she'd landed it into the right spot before depressing the plunger.

"Lady, I really think we need to call an ambulance," he said, his once-calm voice now sounding about as shaky as her nerve endings felt.

"I'll be good as new in a second." She made a circle with her finger and her thumb in the universal signal for A-OK. "The insulin will help even everything out."

He kneeled on the pavement next to her, and she heard the hearty exhale of breath leaving his mouth. "Are you sure you're going to be all right?"

"I'm feeling better already." And it was true. She was. But Molly knew from the last time her blood sugar had spiked like this, it would take a little while to return to normal. She looked at the pulse jumping inside his neck and felt a wave of guilt wash over her. If this was how a complete stranger reacted to her hyperglycemia attack, how would her sister react? Or the rest of her family?

"Sorry for scaring you," she added, more resolved than ever to keep her recent diagnosis a secret. "I would've been fine on my own."

"You sure didn't look fine." His head slumped back against the open car door behind him, then he scrubbed a hand over his lower face. A handsome face actually. The trendy glasses made him look scholarly, but the square jawline made him look determined. Like he wasn't willing to leave her alone until he knew all the answers. "Does that happen often?"

Molly wished she knew. It wasn't like the time she got chicken pox, the itchy red scabs on her torso a constant reminder that she was sick. Curbing her sugar intake was tough enough, but remembering to stay on top of her glucose levels was even trickier since most of the time she felt perfectly fine. As a pilot, Molly had to be "combat ready" at all times. Sometimes she was on duty for twenty-four to forty-eight hours straight, which meant there was no way to ensure that she could eat on a certain schedule to maintain her insulin coverage. The military wasn't going risk both a multi-million-dollar plane and the flight crew because the pilot had hypoglycemia. Everything was still so unpredictable when it came to the disease she'd officially been diagnosed with over a month ago. According to the specialists, that unpredictability meant she could no longer do the only thing she loved.

She drew in a ragged breath and shrugged. "I'm still new to the wonderful world of diabetes."

"Wait. Why would you eat that much sugar if you're diabetic?" His expression looked the same as if he'd just asked, *Why in the world would you pull the pin out of that perfectly good grenade?*

"Because the guy behind the counter said it was healthy."

"And you take nutritional advice from a kid who isn't even old enough to shave?"

Kid! The realization made her scalp tingle and she felt her eyelids stretching wide open. She was officially the worst babysitter in the world.

"I need to get to the ballpark. Now."

"Lady, you're in no shape to be driving right now, let alone playing ball." Kaleb Chatterson adjusted his glasses while slipping the car key he still held into the front pocket of his hoodie. Normally, he had an army of assistants and interns he could've sent to the local grocery store to pick up the ingredients for his dad's margaritas. But he'd needed a break from his parents' nosy questions about his social life and his brothers' incessant teasing about the lack of one.

Coming to the aid of some strange woman in the middle of a medical crisis wasn't exactly what he'd anticipated when he'd volunteered for the errand.

"I'm not the one playing." She rolled her eyes, which were a deep shade of blue. "My nephew is. I'm supposed to pick him up from baseball practice at 1630."

Kaleb noted her use of military time and filed that nugget of information in the back of his mind. "How long does it usually take for you to recover from one of these, um, episodes?"

"Well, last time it took a couple of hours, but I got the insulin dose sooner this time so half that, maybe?"

Kaleb's stomach balled into a knot. He'd once had a crate of antibacterial hand sanitizer delivered to the office when several employees came down with a minor cold. He didn't do sickness or injuries or anything that might hint at the human body's susceptibility to disease. He most assuredly was *not* the person to go to in a medical crisis. And while it seemed as though the lady now had a decent handle on her situation, he would feel a lot more at ease if they had a second opinion. "Listen, my brother's fiancée is a doctor. Let me call her and she can drive over and check you out."

Or check *him* out. Luckily, his adrenaline was pumping his blood around so hard he wasn't likely to faint. Hopefully. He stayed squatted down, close to the ground. Just in case.

"No way. Especially not here where everyone in town would see me."

He eyed the barcode sticker on the rear window of her car, a sure sign that it was a rental. "Are you a local?"

"God, no. I'm just in town visiting my sister and her family. What about you?"

"I'm from Seattle. So if you're not from here, what does it matter if someone sees you?"

"Long story and I'm about to be late." She pulled up her blousy sleeve and looked at the sturdy chronograph watch. Her hand and forearm were equally tan, but a thin line of skin around her ring finger was strikingly white.

Telling himself that he wasn't one of his comic-book heroes and the lady beside him probably wouldn't like being considered a damsel in distress, Kaleb did what he always did when he was out of his league. He pulled out his phone, tapped on the voice to text feature and spoke into the speaker. "Angela, find out how to recover from low blood sugar."

"High blood sugar," the woman corrected him. Yeah, that made more sense considering how much she ate at once.

"Make that *high* blood sugar," he said into the phone, then nodded toward her lap. "Would you mind putting that thing away?"

"What, this?" She lifted up the object and Kaleb felt the color drain out of his face. "It's just a needle. You're not afraid of it, are you?"

"It looks like someone attached a syringe to Dr. Who's sonic screwdriver."

A blank look crossed her face. "What's a sonic screwdriver?"

"Sorry. Geek reference." An embarrassing flush normally would've brought his color back with a vengeance after that less-than-cool admission, but he was woozily watching her put the cap back on her insulin pen and zip it up in its case.

After several uncomfortable moments, the lady next to him broke the silence. "Who's Angela?"

"One of my assistants."

"Just one of them?"

He was saved from having to respond to her sarcastic question by the pinging of his phone. Several texts full of copied and pasted information flooded his screen.

"Hold on," Kaleb said as he read.

However, he was easily distracted by the woman beside him. Now that her color was returning, he could see that there was an edge to her girl-next-door appearance, an attitude that implied she wouldn't back down from a fight. She opened a bottle of water sitting in her center console and chugged it until the plastic concaved into itself. Then she used the back of her hand to wipe the dampness from her mouth. "Angela certainly is fast."

He nodded. That was why he paid her the second highest salary in his company. "Okay, so it says here that, depending on the levels, it can take one to several hours to feel better. She's also suggesting you drink more water and then eat something high in protein and complex carbs once your blood glucose levels return to a normal range."

"An hour? I can't very well sit out here in my car until I'm feeling better. Would you mind giving me a ride?"

"To the ER?" He felt his calf muscles clench, making him eager to stand up and run in the opposite direction. God, Kaleb hated hospitals more than he hated needles. Having multiple medical procedures during one's adolescence tended to do that to a person.

"No. Just to pick up my nephew."

"Can't you get someone else to pick him up?"

She looked at him as if he'd just asked her to hack into the CIA's router network. "His mom, my sister, left town this weekend on something called a 'babymoon' and put me in charge. I can't very well call her and say, 'Oops, sorry, I forgot to pick up your son because I was in a diabetic crisis.'"

"Actually, that's exactly what you could do. Maybe he can get a ride home with a friend?"

"Right. And then my sister would find out and wonder why I couldn't handle it myself."

Kaleb seriously doubted that this woman slouched on the seat next to him *could* handle it. His heart constricted and his head was heavy, which was why he had to keep it supported against the door behind him as he balanced beside her, their bodies only a few inches apart. He of all people knew what it was like to not want someone—especially an overly concerned family member—to think he was weak or needed help.

Still. He was shocked when she turned those pretty blue eyes on him and asked, "Can *you* give me a ride to the baseball field?"

His throat closed in on itself as if it were the plastic water bottle she'd just drained. He coughed to clear it. "But...you don't know me."

"Hi, I'm Molly."

Instinctively, because his mom had drilled good manners into him, he put his hand out and shook hers. "Kaleb."

"Good. Now we know each other."

"But you don't know if I'm a criminal," he argued.

"I know that you're the type to rush to aid a stranger, which means you have a hero complex."

"Ha," he snorted. His brothers would argue that he was the least heroic of all of them, or at least the most self-absorbed. "Maybe I have a villain complex and you're too weak to have figured it out yet."

"I am *not* weak." Her piercing look sent a chill down the back of his neck. He'd always associated the name Molly with a lovable cocker spaniel. But right this second, she looked more like a pissed-off Chihuahua. "Besides, a villain would've already robbed me or kidnapped me by now. And bad guys don't have trusty assistants named Angela."

"So you're the expert on bad guys?" Why was he arguing with her about this? *Just tell her you don't want to give her a ride.* Because he suddenly found himself actually wanting to take her anywhere she needed to go. She looked so delicate and fragile, yet he had a feeling there was a spine of steel under that petite frame. Plus, she was a mystery, a riddle, and he didn't like leaving things unsolved.

"If you'd met my ex, you'd quickly figure out that I'm definitely not an expert on jerks." He raised a brow at that little admission and she clamped her eyes shut. "God, forget I said that."

Too late. Kaleb never forgot anything.

"Sir," a cashier with salt-and-pepper dreadlocks called as she crossed the parking lot. "You forgot your ice and your limes."

"Oh, geez, don't let anyone see me like this." Molly slouched lower in the seat. Great, now she was a cowering Chihuahua. "They'll tell my sister."

Kaleb sighed and stood up. He jogged toward the cashier, trying to meet her halfway.

"Thanks, Donae," he said, reading the name tag on her apron. His father always said that people gave better service when you used their first name. Kaleb usually avoided the practice because it tended to invite familiarity when he was usually trying to keep the public from recognizing him. But he had a feeling he'd need all the allies he could get if he was going to survive the next ten days in this small town.

Kaleb took the dripping bag from Donae's hand and set it down on the asphalt. He reached into his back pocket and pulled out his wallet. "Listen, my friend isn't feeling well and she left her shopping cart in aisle eight. Would you mind ringing those things up and throwing in a liter of water and one of the prewrapped turkey sandwiches from the deli section?"

"No problem, Mr. Chatterson," she replied. Ugh, that was why he didn't do familiarity. It gave strangers the impression that they knew him, which was fine if they'd limit their long-winded conversations to his work life and not to which model or actress or pop singer he'd recently dated. Fortunately, Donae only gave him a wide smile and took the large bills he passed her. "And just so you know, your sister, Kylie, called the store a couple of minutes ago asking if you'd left yet. I told her you were on your way. You want me to call her back?"

His jaw went stiff and he fought off the urge to pinch the bridge of his nose. Just like that, one mention of his awaiting family cemented Kaleb's decision on whether he was going to give cute, determined Molly a ride to get her nephew. "Would you mind telling my sister something came up and I have to help out a friend?"

Okay, so "friend" was a generous description. In fact, Kaleb sincerely doubted his new acquaintance wouldn't have already blasted out of the parking lot without so much as a wave if he hadn't pocketed her car keys.

He hefted the ice into the bed of his dad's lifted, half-ton truck, knowing he'd have to stop somewhere and get another bag before returning to his sister's. Wiping a wet hand on his pant leg, he walked to Molly's car to check on her. She was dozing in the passenger seat and he wondered if he should wake her up. No. That was for concussions, not diabetes. At least he thought so. Hell, he was a software developer, not a doctor. And he certainly wasn't a damn taxi driver.

But a few minutes later, when the cashier pushed out a cart of bagged groceries, he told Donae to keep the change before loading them in the back of Molly's hatchback.

Kaleb was often reminded of the fact that he was the shortest of all the Chatterson brothers, yet he still had to slide the driver's seat back to accommodate his six-foot frame. He started the car and the stereo shot to life. If the booming bass of hip-hop wasn't loud enough to wake Molly up, the vibration of the cheap speakers through the vinyl seats would've done the trick.

"This is for when your levels stabilize." He tossed the wrapped sandwich on her lap and asked, "So how do I get to the baseball park from here?"

## Chapter Two

"This bread has seeds in it," Molly said as she examined the turkey sandwich he'd given her. She was already dehydrated and couldn't afford to use the little saliva she could muster to swallow some tasteless looking cardboard.

"It's whole grain." Kaleb spoke slowly, as though he was explaining jet propulsion to a kindergartner. "It's one of those complex carbs you're supposed to eat once you drink enough fluid to flush out all the excess sugar from your system."

Her unsolicited rescuer was sure turning out to be quite the know-it-all.

"I'm well aware of what I'm supposed to be eating and drinking." As if to prove it, she took another long swig of the water he'd thoughtfully purchased after she'd already downed an entire bottle.

"Forgive me for doubting that when I overheard you asking some clueless teenager at the juice bar if the strawberry-banana smoothie was low in sugar."

"Well, I *will* be aware. As soon as I meet with the nutritionist at Shadowview." Molly actually had several appointments at the nearby military hospital, but she'd been putting them off. She could only handle one tailspin at a time.

"So you *are* in the military." It was more of a statement than a question.

Technically, she was. But she didn't know for how much longer. Ever since the flight surgeon wrote up a medical board determining that her recently diagnosed condition made her ineligible to fly, Molly had refused to think about where her career was headed. So instead, she changed the subject. "You can stop looking at the map on your phone. I know where we're going."

"But my GPS is saying it's quicker to take Snowflake Boulevard to Lake Street."

"Does your GPS also say that Lake Street is blocked off today because the high school drill team is practicing for next week's Sun Potato Parade?"

"Hmpf." His hand reluctantly dropped the fancy high-tech device into the center console, then loosely gripped it, as though he might need to grab it again at any second. "It probably would if there was a Sun Potato Parade app available to download."

"You can talk to my nephew about inventing one. He lives for dorky tech stuff like that." Molly saw Kaleb's hand clench tighter around his phone and she wondered what she could've said to annoy him. If she wasn't so exhausted, she might've asked him. She pointed to the next stop sign. "Make a left up here."

"Speaking of your nephew, won't he think there's something wrong if you show up with a stranger?"

"I'll tell him I had too much to drink." She felt the deceleration of the car before she realized he'd completely taken his foot off the gas pedal. She let her head roll to the side, which was a mistake since it only afforded her a full view of his handsome—and doubt-filled—face.

"You'd rather people think you were drunk than diabetic?" His incredulous tone hit her in the belly with a force. Or maybe she was still sore from where she'd given herself that shot. "Are you seriously that desperate to keep this from your family?"

"*Desperate* is a strong word," she said cautiously. In fact, it sounded a lot like *weak*. And she was neither. "I'm simply protecting them from worrying about me. And I didn't mean alcohol. His mom warned him not to have too much soda this weekend because it would give him a bellyache. So I was going to go that route."

He made a weird mumbling sound as he pulled into the parking lot. All the other kids must've already been picked up because poor Hunter was the only boy waiting by the bleachers. She curled her fingers into her palm, unable to release the guilt building inside her. Molly came from a big, busy family with at least one parent usually off on deployment. Getting forgotten at school or left behind at soccer practice was an all too familiar feeling and she hated that her condition was now affecting others.

She leaped out of the passenger door before Kaleb had even put the car in Park. Well, she didn't leap so much as stumble on shaky legs, feeling as if she'd just stepped onto solid ground after a ten-hour flight in a cramped cockpit.

"Sorry I'm so late, buddy," she said, wrapping her twelve-year-old nephew into a bear hug, made all the more awkward by the fact that he'd shot up a couple inches taller than her this past winter and was carrying a duffel bag in one hand and a batting helmet in the other. As well as by the fact that she'd just seen him less than two hours ago. "Have you been waiting all by yourself?"

"No problem, Aunt Molly. Practice has only been done a few minutes and Coach Russell is still here chalking the base lines for tomorrow's game." Hunter untangled himself from her overzealous greeting and opened the rear door to toss his gear into the back seat. "Hey! You didn't tell me Kaleb was coming with you!"

"Hunter, my man," Kaleb said casually as he pivoted in the driver's seat and did a complicated fist bump with her nephew.

"What?" Molly fumbled with the door handle. "You guys know each other?"

"Pfshhh," Hunter responded. "Anyone living in the twenty-first century knows Kaleb Chatterson."

"Oh, hell." She inspected her grocery store hero through squinted eyes. "You're a Chatterson?"

"That's another dollar for my swear jar, Aunt Molly."

"According to my birth certificate." Kaleb shrugged, then put the car into gear. "The DNA tests are still in question."

A throb started in her temples and Molly had to wonder if her visit to Sugar Falls could get any worse. She pulled her wallet out and tossed a ten dollar bill onto Hunter's lap. "Consider me paid up until Sunday."

\* \* \*

"But you said you were from Seattle," Molly accused through gritted teeth as she latched her seat belt.

"I am." Kaleb was doing *her* a favor. Why was *he* the one being put on the defensive? "And would you mind telling me where I'm supposed to take you?"

"I'm staying at my sister's apartment. But I guess you knew that all along."

Whoa. This lady was coming at him with guns blazing. If that wasn't discomforting enough, a twelve-year-old kid had his seat belt stretched to the limits as he practically leaned between their two seats, not wanting to miss a minute of the action. "How in the world would I have known that? I didn't have a clue who you were until fifteen minutes ago."

In fact, it wasn't until Kaleb heard Hunter call her "Aunt Molly" that the puzzle began clicking together. The woman beside him must somehow be related to Maxine, who was best friends with his sister, Kylie. But he was still missing the pieces that explained why she was suddenly so annoyed with him.

"But you know me, right, Kaleb?" Hunter's voice cracked and it didn't take a rearview mirror for Kaleb to know the kid's eager freckled face was only inches behind his own. "Remember when we were at your sister's wedding last year and you promised me an internship at your company when I turned eighteen?"

Kaleb squeezed his eyes shut briefly. How could he forget? Of course, he would've called it a surrender more than a promise since, at the time, Hunter was the only person who'd been able to smuggle in a tablet—despite Kylie's ban of all electronic devices at the reception—and

Kaleb's Tokyo office was in the middle of negotiations to buy out a company that built virtual-reality headsets.

Yet, before anyone could comment on the circumstances surrounding the supposed internship, the kid's aunt interrupted. "If you're from Seattle, then what are you doing in Sugar Falls?"

As he turned onto Snowflake Boulevard, which could've just as easily been named Main Street, USA, he took in the grassy park in the center of downtown to assure himself that they were still in a free country. "The same thing you are. Visiting family."

She mumbled an expletive under her breath and he was pretty sure that, at this rate, Hunter was going to have enough money in his swear jar to get him through the first two years of college.

"Speaking of *family*." Kaleb emphasized the last word to remind her her children were present. "Does your sister still live above her shop?"

"Not anymore," Hunter answered for his aunt, who was silently fuming in the front seat. "We moved out to a bigger house when she and Cooper got married. But Aunt Molly is staying there while she's in town. She says it's because she doesn't want to be in our way, but Mom says it's because she doesn't want us knowing her business."

Molly gasped before turning in her seat to look at her nephew. "Your mom told you that?"

Hunter had his palms up. "Not in a bad way or nothin'… She said all the Markhams are like that."

"So where are we going?" Kaleb interrupted. If he wanted a front-row seat to watch family members bickering, he'd head back to his sister's house and watch his own brothers argue over who got to man the back-yard grill.

"To the apartment over the bakery." Molly sighed. Even an outsider like Kaleb knew that when some-one said *bakery* in this town, they actually meant the Sugar Falls Cookie Company. "It shouldn't be that far of a walk for you to get back to your car at Duncan's Market."

Not that far? It was at least a mile through town and both his phone and his watch—he never should've synced the two—currently sounded like winning slot machines with unanswered texts from his dad and his sister, probably wanting to know where the heck he was with their ice and limes.

"Why's your car at Duncan's?" Hunter asked. So far they'd avoided having to explain why he was driving them home, but if the kid was as observant as Kaleb had been at that age, it didn't take a computer genius to figure out Molly was hiding something.

"Because your aunt had a—"

"Wait." Molly pointed a finger his way. "Which Chatterson brother are you?"

"I'm Kaleb," he said slowly, second-guessing his earlier decision to go along with her pleas to not seek medical assistance.

"I caught the name." Her eyes were narrowed into slits. "I meant are you one of the baseball Chattersons or are you the one who plays video games for a living?"

Despite being on the cover of *Forbes* last month for their feature article on "World's Youngest Billionaires," Kaleb's siblings never let him forget that no matter how much money he made, he would always be the little brother. So when Molly said "video games" in that tone,

she might as well have been asking if he was the one
who set fire to small wildlife animals in his parents'
basement. At least his back brace and teenage acne
were long gone. Along with his self-respect apparently.

"Video games?" Hunter snorted. "Kaleb's, like, the
most successful software developer in the world."

Oblivious to the tension in the front seat, the boy
launched into a monologue about the company's top-
selling games while Molly's eyes shot icy glares at
Kaleb and her forefinger made a dramatic swipe against
her throat. It took him a moment to figure out that she
was referring to him staying silent about what had happened at the store, not his job profession. Or maybe she
didn't want him to bring up either subject. All he knew
was that he liked her soft pink lips a lot more when they
weren't pursed together in a violent shushing gesture.
Actually, he kind of liked them both ways.

He mouthed the words, "What's the big deal?"

But the minivan behind him honked to let him
know the light had changed to green, and he didn't get
a chance to lip-read Molly's response.

So she had diabetes. What was the big deal? Millions
of people probably had the same diagnosis and didn't
go into undercover stealth mode to keep it a secret. He
needed to know why.

"Dude, all of your electronic devices are, like, going
crazy." Hunter was apparently done with his rambling
soliloquy about Perfect Game Industries, although it did
give Kaleb's ego a boost to know that at least one person in the town of Sugar Falls—besides his mother—
didn't think his company was a fallback career. "Are
you gonna answer them?"

Kaleb glanced at the display. Speaking of his mother,

his family was certainly busting out the big guns if Lacey Chatterson was trying to track him down. Everyone knew he never avoided his mom's calls. If he didn't respond soon, he'd get a firsthand look at how this little ski resort town up in the mountains ran a full-scale search party.

"I'll call them back later," he said, slipping his cell phone into his front pocket. "Let's help your aunt take these groceries inside."

Falling completely off the grid and being the irresponsible Chatterson might be fun for a change.

## Chapter Three

When Molly had initially been medically grounded, she'd still been living on base so the daily routine of military life made it easy to pretend that nothing would change. Just like the time she'd twisted her ankle after a postejection survival training exercise, she pulled office duty—pushing paperwork and keeping her personal life classified. There was no point in getting her family and squad mates all worried about something that would probably require a simple fix. She hadn't even told her fiancé about her diagnosis. Although, in her defense, she'd been about to when she walked into Trevor's condo with a bag of Chinese takeout from his favorite restaurant and found him eating pork dumplings from the ends of another woman's chopsticks.

Canceling vendors, returning wedding gifts and watching her savings account free-fall with all the forfeited deposits was only slightly more pleasant than undergoing a battery of doctor appointments and lab tests. In a last-ditch attempt to get away from it all, Molly had cashed in on Trevor's trip insurance and went solo on the honeymoon that never was. Unfortunately, besides a great suntan and a somewhat functional straw tote from a street market in Fiji, Molly's head wasn't any clearer than it had been two weeks ago.

As she looked around at her sister's apartment—which she'd been thinking of as her temporary duty station until she could figure out what she was going to do with her life—Molly felt as though she'd just overshot her landing and had to circle around and try it again. Exhausted, both emotionally and physically, she was halfway curled into a ball on the oversize white sofa in the living room, watching her nephew and Kaleb put away groceries she didn't remember selecting. What in the world was she going to do with all those cans of soup?

More important, what was she going to do with this guy who now knew her secret? She shuddered. Even thinking the word *secret* made her feel all dirty and cowardly, like she was hunkering down in some barren cave rather than Maxine's plush renovated apartment in the heart of quaint, touristy Sugar Falls.

Kaleb's face was so handsome the glasses almost looked fake. A few weeks ago, when she'd first experienced problems with dizziness, Molly had been looking at all the advertisement posters above the display cases at the ophthalmologist's office while she waited for her vision tests to come back. This guy resembled the sexy models in the pictures, trying to convince the middle-aged patients with cataracts and receding hairlines that they, too, would look like some gorgeous stud if only they invested in the right spectacles.

His brown hair was a bit too long and too messy. His jeans were a bit too new and too expensive, despite the fact that they certainly fit his slim hips well. And when he'd stripped off his hooded sweatshirt and she'd seen him in his shirt, Molly let out a breath she didn't know she'd been holding. His dark blue T-shirt appeared to be made for him, the fabric so soft and well-worn she could see the ridges of his lean muscles under it.

All in all, he didn't look like the owner of a multi-billion-dollar technology empire. Which was probably why she was so surprised to find out that he was related to her sister's best friend. Not that the rest of the Chattersons were much different than this one, with the exception of most of them being redheads. And they were only millionaires, as opposed to billionaires.

"Can we order some pizza from Patrelli's?" Hunter asked after digging around in the shopping bags and only coming up with food that would require a can opener to prepare.

She nodded and would've handed him her cell phone, but he'd already pulled out his own. "Get me a large meatball sub," she said as he started dialing.

"Actually," Kaleb interjected, "Molly is going to have the chicken Caesar salad. Dressing on the side."

Hunter gave his idol a thumbs-up before speaking to a person on the other end of the line. Apparently, being a favorite aunt had just been trumped by the guy who invented some stupid video game called "Blockcraft."

"But I wanted the meatball sub." Molly crossed her arms across her chest, her voice sounding whinier than she'd intended.

"And do you also want your nephew to have to call 9-1-1 when you go into another one of your blood sugar attacks?" One of Kaleb's brown eyebrows arched above his glasses.

Molly tried to arch her own brow in response to him, but only succeeded in looking like she had something stuck in her eye. Being tired was one thing, but she was beginning to feel completely useless.

"I'm gonna walk down the block to pick it up," Hunter said, pulling on a sweatshirt. "I sure like our new house, but sometimes I really miss living in the middle of town like this."

Kaleb handed the boy two twenty-dollar bills and her nephew was out the door before Molly could even protest. Or ask him not to leave her alone with the hunky tech guy who'd just saved her. Sort of.

"You didn't have to buy dinner, too. I have money," she said, looking around for her wallet. Actually, she didn't know how much longer her military salary would last and she probably shouldn't be wasting it on pizza—or dry salads, in this case.

"I think all of your cash went to the swear jar," Kaleb said, his hands loosely tucked into his front pockets. He was probably eager to get away from her. Not that she could blame him. She'd been trying to get away from herself for quite a few weeks, as well.

His watch rang again, or was it his phone? Nope, this time it was his cell. Picking it up from the counter, he said, "I really need to take this."

"Okay, but if it's your sister, don't tell her about… you know…"

"Why not?"

"Because then she'll tell *my* sister, remember?"

He rolled his eyes, then swiped his finger across the screen. "Hey, Kylie."

Molly dragged her tote bag onto her lap and pulled out her black case. She may as well check her glucose levels before Hunter returned. The distraction might also keep her from listening to Kaleb's smooth, deep voice.

As she pricked her finger and pressed out a droplet of blood, she heard him make several noncommittal sounds to whatever his sister was saying on the other end.

"Mmm-hmm." He walked around the coffee table to stand beside her, the waistband of his jeans right in her line of vision. Lately, in the guy department, Molly thought she'd been working on autopilot. However, a shot of electricity zipped through her, activating the dormant wiring circuits in her lower extremities.

"Uh-huh." He leaned over to see the digital reading on her compact machine. She tightened her lips, taking in a deep breath through her nose. Whoa. Did all billionaires smell this amazing?

"Is that good?" he whispered to her, his hand over the speaker and his eyes soft with concern. She had to force her own eyes away from his flat abdomen and toward the numbers on the screen in front of her.

She was almost back within normal range, yet still gave him an "okay" sign with her thumb and forefinger. His smile mirrored the relief she should have felt. Or would have felt if her heart hadn't started hammering at how close he was to her.

"No, Molly's fine." His voice snapped her brain out of whatever trance she'd just been in and she began waving her arms in front of her face, inadvertently hitting him in the hip and causing him to glare down at her.

"Don't say my name," she whispered.

"Too late," he mouthed.

"Here, let me talk to her." She reached for his phone, but her energy hadn't fully recovered and her crisscrossed legs got tangled when she tried to stand up. He sidestepped her and held his palm out, probably trying to cut her off because he thought he had the conversation under control.

"No, she wasn't too sloshed to drive," Kaleb told his sister indignantly.

Molly gave him a nod of encouragement. "Yeah, let's go with that."

"Oh, c'mon, Kylie. I'm not going to ask her if she's pregnant."

Hmm. Molly tilted her head to the side and tapped a couple of fingers against her lip. As far as red herrings went, it wasn't ideal. But she could work with it. Maxine knew about the breakup with Trevor and Molly hadn't exactly corrected her sister when she'd offered up the use of her apartment as a refuge for mending her broken heart. Pregnancy definitely would be a lot simpler to explain, at least for a few months while she bought herself more time.

"Because it's none of my business," Kaleb said into the phone. "And it's none of yours."

Molly's eyes widened in surprise. She couldn't believe that he was jumping to her defense, but she nodded her encouragement, anyway.

"Uh-huh." Kaleb pushed his hair off his forehead, then ran a hand through his dark brown curls, which fell in waves to his chin. "Fine. I'll be there in thirty minutes and we can talk about it then."

Molly collapsed backward, her head falling into a pile of down throw pillows. It would've been nice if he could've stalled a bit more. As it was, she would now have half that time to coach Kaleb on exactly what to say to throw his family off her trail. Or to figure out a way to prevent him from walking out of this apartment.

"No, you do not need to send Dad to come get me." Kaleb spoke into the phone, but he was staring straight at Molly. And his annoyed expression promised retribution for this farce she'd gotten them both into.

When he arrived at Kylie's house a while later, Kaleb surrendered the margarita fixings and tried to give his incredibly nosy family the look that usually sent his employees scurrying back to their cubicles. Or at least the look he intended to convey his authority and his unwillingness to discuss a matter. Unfortunately, his family didn't work for him and they certainly didn't respect any boundaries when it came to his personal life—or any facet of his life, really.

"Maybe you should've called one of her relatives," his mother suggested.

"Or brought her here so we could check her out ourselves," Kylie advised.

"You mean interrogate her in person?" Kaleb asked, and his sister rolled her eyes in response. "You guys, she was totally fine. It's probably some twenty-four-hour bug that's going around. In fact, I should probably quarantine myself in case I was exposed. Wouldn't want to get any of you sick."

"Nice try, Brainiac," Kylie replied. "As if Captain

Markham would be felled by some pesky flu. That woman is as tough as they come. Maxine told me that one time, when Molly was in flight school, she got her thumb stuck in a busted air shaft vent and almost ripped it clean off. Rather than tell her instructors or call for a medic, she used her good hand and a utility knife and cut off the strap of her bra to hold the digit in place. She would've cut into the fabric of her flight suit, but she didn't want to be out of uniform."

"Still," his mom said. "You probably shouldn't have left her alone if she's sick."

Kaleb had told himself that same thing during his walk back to the truck at Duncan's, during his wait at the checkout line at the market with a fresh—and unmelted—bag of ice and then throughout the entire drive here. "She was already feeling better when I left and she's not alone. She's with her nephew. And trust me, that kid is smart enough to call in for reinforcements even if his stubborn aunt isn't."

"So, you think Molly's stubborn?" His sister's eyes lit up and Kaleb knew from experience not to let her bait him.

"No, *you* said she was stubborn when she tried to fix her own thumb instead of getting help."

"I said she was tough, not stubborn."

"What's the difference?" Kaleb asked, then thought better of his question when he saw both his sister and his mom open their mouths to answer him. "Never mind. Listen, I'm gonna head over to Kane's house just in case I caught whatever bug Molly has. I'll call you guys in the morning."

Kaleb knew full well that what Molly had wasn't contagious, but if it got him out of the line of fire quicker, he'd say whatever he could to get a few hours' reprieve. And in his defense, he was doing it to protect her. To protect her secret. He wasn't avoiding his family because they drove him nuts. Truly.

Although, if his relatives even got the slightest suspicion that he, in any way, was attracted to an eligible woman, the teasing would never cease. Not that Molly was eligible. Or that Kaleb cared either way. Dating led to obligations and obligations led to commitment. The only commitment he had time for was his company.

On the drive to his brother's house—where he was staying alone since Kane had moved into town with his fiancée—Kaleb picked up his smartphone several times to call Molly and check on her, each time realizing he never got her phone number. He'd programmed his number into her cell and told her to call him in case anything came up. But she'd never offered to do the same.

Which was for the best. He had no business calling her, let alone fostering this bizarre sense of responsibility he now felt toward her. When he'd dealt with scoliosis, he'd hated people babying him, wondering if the brace he wore was uncomfortable, telling him he'd be able to play sports again soon enough. Kaleb couldn't imagine she'd respond any differently than he had as a surly teenager, determined to prove to the world that he was just as healthy and capable as everyone else in his athletic family.

But the silence of the truck cab felt unnatural, as did the feeling of not being on the phone with someone. So Kaleb used his voice command feature to call his assistant. He counted three rings, more than the usual two, before Angela answered.

"You're supposed to be on vacation," Angela said by way of greeting.

"I'm never on vacation."

"Does your old man know that?" his assistant asked. "Because Coach Chatterson gave me very specific instructions that nobody from the office was to bother you for the next ten days while you're with your family."

That was just like his father to go behind his back like that. And with one of his trusted employees, no less. "Does my dad pay your salary now?"

"No, but he promised to get me a baseball signed by your brother if I sent all the employees a memo instructing them not to call you."

"Sellout," Kaleb snorted.

"Can you blame me? Do you know how much authenticated memorabilia signed by the infamous Kane Chatterson goes for nowadays?"

"I didn't mean *you*. I meant my brother. He of all people should know not to interfere in my business."

"Aw, c'mon, Kaleb. You told your family that the only way you would take time off from *your* job was if they agreed to take time off *their* jobs. You can't blame them for wanting to get you back for scheduling this trip right during the middle of baseball season."

He grunted, but smiled to himself because he'd definitely outplayed his dad and brothers with that negotiation maneuver.

"Besides," Angela continued, "deep down, you know your family is looking out for your best interest."

"Story of my life," Kaleb said as he flicked on the turn signal. A few years ago, he would've been annoyed, but now the high-handed move was completely expected and Kaleb would've suspected something was wrong if his family *hadn't* tried to protect him in some way. Old habits were hard to break and all that. He didn't begrudge them their motivation, even when he grew exasperated with their tactics. "So, tell me how the testing of the avatar prototype went."

"It went great for the preliminary rounds. A couple of minor glitches to work out but our software team is on top of it."

"Have them meet with the graphic artists to go over—"

"They're already on it, Boss Man," Angela interrupted.

"What about the negotiations with the record label to let us use that song for the intro to 'Zombies vs. Alien Pirates'?"

"The legal department is drawing up the contracts this week."

He made a right turn onto the long dirt driveway leading to the house Kane had refurbished last year. Kaleb wasn't ready to call it a night quite yet, though. An unexplained restlessness simmered in his belly and he reached for his tablet on the passenger seat. He pulled up his electronic calendar on the screen as he steered the truck with one hand. "Where are we at with those new health care benefits for the administration staff?"

"They decided that they'd rather have a sushi chef in the cafeteria than affordable insurance, so HR is actively screening applicants at every Japanese restaurant in the greater Seattle area."

"Really?" Kaleb jerked his head up, stopping in front of the barn that had been converted into a garage.

"No, Kaleb. Not really. But I left a very good-looking

date and a warm cup of sake so I could step outside of Sensei Miso's and take your call."

Angela had been the first person Kaleb hired when he'd started Perfect Game Industries, which meant that she'd been with him since before he could legally drink alcohol and, therefore, felt free to give him her opinion—along with any other unsolicited advice she deemed suitable. Funny how in his quest to start a business that was completely independent of his family, he hired the one person who acted like his long-lost big sister all the time.

Which was probably why he sounded less like an authoritative boss and more like a petulant little brother when he replied, "You could've said as much when you answered the phone."

"Kaleb, you and I both know that my salary more than compensates me for these after-hours calls. But you're supposed to be on vacation. That means that all your vice presidents and department directors are getting a vacation from you micromanaging us."

"I've never micromanaged anyone in my life," Kaleb shot back, using his finger to scroll through his online notes to see if there was anything he'd missed regarding the marketing staff.

"Whatever you say, Boss Man." Angela's tone wasn't the least bit deferential.

"You don't know micromanagement until you've spent a day with the Chatterson family."

"If that's an invitation, I'm calling the company pilot right now and telling him to fuel up the Gulfstream."

"Perfect. Tell him that when he drops you off, he can take me back with him. Actually, bring that new admin assistant from accounting with you. I hear he's been angling for your job since he started. I bet he'll be glad to know that the position is finally opening up."

"You mean the one who wore the Bobby Chatterson retro jersey to the company roller-skating party last month? Yeah, I'm sure he wouldn't be above taking a bribe from your old man, either."

"Are you done with the sarcasm?" Kaleb asked. If he wanted to deal with people giving him a hard time, he'd drive back to Kylie's house. Or even to Molly's. How did he always inevitably surround himself with so many know-it-all women?

"You started it," Angela pointed out. "Seriously, though, Kaleb. You've hired the best of the best to work for you. The least you could do is trust us to handle things while you enjoy your vacation."

Kaleb would hardly call this trip to Sugar Falls a vacation. He'd much rather be at the office dealing with things himself, rather than delegating. But he'd made a promise to his parents to at least try.

Just like he'd made a promise to a petite, blue-eyed blonde that he'd keep her secret safe. He looked at the digital calendar on his smartwatch. Nine more days to go.

## Chapter Four

Molly had only been in Sugar Falls for seventy-two hours, and already she knew why the locals didn't go to the restaurants on the weekends. She took a tentative sip of her coffee minus the cream and sugar—thank you very much, unreliable pancreas—as Hunter swiveled in the counter stool next to her, trying to locate a customer he might know from school or the Little League field.

"Man, this place is packed for a Monday!" Her nephew seemed intent on not using his inside voice.

"It's Memorial Day weekend, bud." She handed him one of the laminated menus with the Cowgirl Up Café logo printed on the front.

"I told you we shoulda gone to the Donut Stop. At least there we could've run into someone we actually know."

Yeah, that was the exact reason why Molly'd shot down his suggestion first thing this morning. Well, that and the fact that she wouldn't have been able to order anything other than a starchy, cream-filled sugar bomb. She hadn't been back to Duncan's Market since Friday and Hunter had already exhausted the supply of left-over pizza for his past two breakfasts.

She was supposed to be the fun aunt. The aunt with no rules. The aunt who all the nieces and nephews begged to come chaperone their school dances or to take them and their friends on tours of Blackhawk helicopters. Or at least she would have been if she ever spent some quality time with any of them.

She'd like to think she'd been mostly fun this weekend, going hiking and kayaking and bike riding. But she'd also been feeding her growing twelve-year-old nephew a steady diet of canned soup, which was about the least exciting thing on the planet to eat.

"Finally!" Hunter all but shouted over the noise of the crowded restaurant. "Hey, Kaleb, there's a spot right here!"

Molly's shoulders froze, her coffee mug suspended halfway between the Formica counter and her clenched jaw. She should've gone to the Donut Stop and risked a maple-glazed-induced coma. Her pride forbade her from turning around to make eye contact with Kaleb, thereby encouraging him to accept Hunter's invitation to sit by them. But her curiosity told her pride to go pound sand.

That zapping electrical current shot through her body again. She shouldn't have looked.

He was still wearing those serious glasses, paired with jeans that were meant to look sloppy but probably cost more than her officer's mess dress uniform—which was the most expensive thing she owned. His green T-shirt displayed a replica of the blueprints for the *Millennium Falcon*, and Hunter immediately commented on their apparent shared love of *Star Wars* as Kaleb warily approached.

"Are you sure you don't mind me joining you guys?" Given the way his eyes were fixated on her face, he was directing the question toward her.

But Hunter answered before she could. "Heck, no. Hurry up before one of the tourists tries to snake this spot."

The waitress was possibly new, her gaze darting back and forth between the counter and the booths as though she didn't know who to help next. Her turquoise Cowgirl Up Café T-shirt seemed way too tight and didn't go with the long, flowing skirt. Molly remembered her high school job at a fish and chips place near Groton, Connecticut, when her parents had been stationed at the military base there. On her first day, she'd been tossed an oversize orange-and-blue striped polyester dress that smelled like battered grease and Atlantic cod and had the name "Dolores" stenciled on the front.

She felt this woman's pain. Thank God Molly had become a pilot, because she had sucked at every job she'd ever had before enlisting. Ugh! Did that mean that if she couldn't fly planes, she'd have to go back to waitressing? To being around all this delicious food and not being able to sample a single bite?

When Monica—at least that what the waitress's name tag read—finally made her way to them, she fumbled with her notepad and barely made eye contact before asking to take their order.

"You gotta get one of their cinnamon rolls, Aunt Molly," Hunter said. "They're world famous."

"As good as that sounds, I think I'm going to get the veggie omelet." She tried to ignore her nephew's gagging expression.

"Would you like hash browns or home fries with that?" Monica asked.

Even with Hunter sitting between them, and at least fifty other diners in the surrounding area, Molly could clearly hear Kaleb's swift intake of breath. She zeroed in on his disapproving scowl.

"What?" Molly asked.

"Potatoes are a starch, which basically converts into sugar as soon as it hits your digestive tract."

"They're also a vegetable. I'm sure a couple of bites would be fine."

"Look." Kaleb pointed to something on the menu before suggesting, "How about the sliced tomatoes?"

The waitress, who, up until that point, had looked as though she'd rather be anywhere that didn't require social interaction, lifted one of her eyebrows at Molly and gave her that look women give each other to silently ask, *Are you really going to let this guy talk to you like that?*

Each fiber of Molly's soul wanted to fight back and order every single potato product they served—which would've been quite a meal considering they were in the great state of Idaho. But she ignored the throbbing vein in her temple and only mildly defied him by forcing out the words, "I'll take the cottage cheese." And then in an effort to prove to this stranger that the controlling man sitting next to them wasn't the boss of her, she added, "And a side of bacon."

When Kaleb ordered the cinnamon roll French toast, Molly shot him the dirtiest look she could manage. It might've been juvenile, but it was either that or risk giving Hunter another IOU for his swear jar.

"I thought you guys were friends," her nephew said once Monica left to get Kaleb's orange juice.

"I don't know if I'd say we were—" Kaleb broke off when Molly drew a finger across her neck.

"Of course we're friends, Hunter." Molly held the tight smile as her nephew looked back and forth between them. She prayed her jaw didn't crack.

"Oh, I get it," the boy finally said. "My mom and Cooper used to argue like that before they got married."

"We're not arguing," Kaleb's mouth said, while his eyes added, *Nor are we getting married.*

Not that she needed him to spell it out. But clearly, Hunter did, because the twelve-year-old didn't look convinced.

"That's also what my mom and Cooper used to say." Hunter's knowing smirk was enough to make Molly sink down in her seat as she bit back an argumentative response.

Oddly enough, that wasn't the most awkward breakfast Kaleb had ever had. Even when he'd grabbed the check, only to have Molly tear the paper in two when she wrestled it out of his grip, he'd only been mildly annoyed. Too bad the business owners in Sugar Falls hadn't caught on to SmartPay; otherwise, he could've paid the bill with a simple tap on his watch.

In fact, the woman seemed to bring out his competitive spirit, a Chatterson trait that always seemed to intensify whenever he was in the same city as his antagonistic siblings. Plus, seeing her get all flustered and defensive every time she thought Kaleb might slip and say something was rather entertaining.

Most of the women he went out with were overly agreeable, always putting him—and his bank account—on a pedestal. Fortunately, the novelty of dating a billionaire wore off as soon as they realized Kaleb spent more time inside his company's headquarters than he did jet-setting around the world, making social appearances. So it was an interesting change of pace to be sharing a meal with an attractive female who wasn't trying to impress him or talk him into taking her shopping or to a swanky, new restaurant.

Actually, Kaleb got the impression that Molly couldn't wait for him to leave. They'd barely walked outside the café when Hunter invited him over to play video games. Kaleb was tempted to accept, if only to see Molly squirm some more.

"I thought we were going to head into Boise today to see that new superhero movie," Molly told her nephew.

"Superhero movie?" Kaleb asked. He knew exactly which one she was talking about because he'd been an adviser on set to Robert Downey, Jr., and had been invited to the premiere a few weeks ago. "Could you be a little more specific?"

"You know." Molly rolled her wrist in a circle. "The one where the guy wears that suit and he fights that bad guy who is trying to destroy that thing."

Hunter slapped a palm to his forehead. "He's called Iron Man." Then the kid looked at Kaleb. "You wanna come with us?"

"I wish I could." And he was surprised to realize that was the truth. He'd love to sit by Molly in a dark air-conditioned movie theater, sharing a hot bucket of buttery popcorn... Wait. Was she supposed to eat popcorn? He pulled out his phone to ask his voice-operated search engine, then saw the two sets of eyes eagerly awaiting his response to the original question. Although each set looked hopeful for opposite answers.

"Actually, I can't," he finally said, and Molly let out the breath she'd been holding. "I'm supposed to go with my family on some sort of ATV tour this afternoon."

Her look of relief suddenly turned to one of blanket envy. He recognized the expression from twenty minutes ago when she was staring at the maple syrup dripping off the cinnamon roll French toast he was eating, looking like she wanted to stab him with her fork so that she could lick his plate clean.

Just then, Hunter waved at a kid getting out of an SUV down the street. "That's Jake Marconi. Hold on a sec, I'm gonna go tell him something."

The boy left Kaleb standing there alone with his aunt.

"I'll give you ten dollars to switch with me this afternoon," Molly said under her breath, her nephew barely out of hearing distance.

"I'd gladly switch for free," Kaleb replied. "But my dad keeps accusing me of avoiding my family. Trust me. I'd much rather see the movie again than bounce along an overgrown trail, hanging on to some four-wheeled motorcycle for dear life."

Her face was incredulous. "Are you kidding? Who'd want to sit and watch a bunch of fake action on the screen when you could be out there living it?"

"Someone who doesn't want to spend the evening on his sister's sofa with a heating pad wedged under his back." Not that Kaleb was worried about a flare-up from his old surgery, but it was obvious that an adrenaline junkie like Molly—or at least like most pilots—wouldn't understand that some people preferred to get their excitement the virtual way.

"Hey, Kaleb." Hunter ran back to them, another boy

on his heels and a woman trying to keep up behind them. "This is my friend Jake. I told him you'd sign his copy of 'Alien Pirates: Martianbeard's Redemption.'"

"Sorry for imposing on you like this," Jake's mother said when she caught up to them. She pulled a plastic case out of her purse. "But my son heard you were in town and has been carrying this video game around in the hopes that we'd run into you and could get your autograph."

"Of course," he said as the mom handed him a Sharpie. He cleared his throat, mostly embarrassed that Molly was watching the entire encounter, but secretly hoping she was slightly impressed. Other women would be, but Molly was turning out to be unlike anyone else he'd ever met.

Mrs. Marconi, as if suddenly realizing someone else was standing there, held out her phone to Molly. "Would you mind taking a picture of us?"

"That's my aunt Molly," Hunter explained to everyone. "You might've seen her when she and Kaleb picked me up at baseball practice on Friday night. We were just having breakfast together."

Even to Kaleb's ears, the kid was laying it on a bit thick with the implications of how well they were acquainted. But he knew how twelve-year-old boys talked when they wanted to impress their friends. Unfortunately, Molly's face turned scarlet and she tried to hide it behind the phone as she held it up for a picture. She didn't even count to three or tell them to say cheese before quickly tapping the shutter and telling Hunter, "C'mon, bud. We better get going if we don't want to be late for that movie."

Kaleb didn't get a chance to say goodbye to her and

was left standing with Jake and his mom, who was possibly an even bigger video game fan than her son. If only his assistant could see him now. Take that, Angela. Some people might want his brothers' autograph on balls and team jerseys, but there were also people in this world who wanted his. Maybe he should call his director of marketing and look into producing more memorabilia.

Unfortunately, death by ATV would be preferable to all the personal questions Mrs. Marconi was soon launching his way. She wanted to know how long he'd be in town and how well he knew Maxine Cooper's sister. Kaleb tried to direct the conversation back to Jake and level eight of "Pirate Space Blasters." After about two minutes—which felt like two hours—he tapped on his watch and said he had an important conference call to get to.

Still driving his dad's truck, Kaleb slowly took the road to his sister's house. He didn't even notice that he hadn't activated his Bluetooth or punched in coordinates onto the navigation screen. He was too busy remembering the way Molly had looked at that syrup, wondering how his body would react if she looked at him the same way. So maybe the breakfast had been a bit awkward. But in a good way.

There definitely could've been worse ways to spend his morning.

When they got back from seeing the movie in Boise, Molly followed Hunter into Maxine and Cooper's house. They'd moved after they found out they were having a baby and would need something bigger than the two-bedroom apartment in town.

Her sister looked even more pregnant than she had on Friday morning when she and Cooper had left town. Hunter didn't seem to mind his mother's increasing belly as she held the boy in a firm hug and told him how much they'd missed him.

Cooper agreed, and when he wrapped his arms around his stepson, he practically lifted the twelve-year-old off his feet. Molly hung back, shifting from her left foot to her right. The Markham family hadn't been big in the demonstrative affection department and Molly never seemed to know what to do when she saw parents openly displaying their love for their kids. Sure, she was technically related to them, but she and Maxine weren't the kind of sisters who got blubbery and emotional whenever they saw each other. As children, they'd been physically close by default. It was difficult not to be when six kids shared two rooms. But all that togetherness only made the Markham siblings anxious to spring out on their own as soon as they hit adulthood.

Being military brats, it wasn't like they'd had a childhood home to go back to, so their visits were few and far between and the distance became more and more natural. Not that Molly was complaining. There were plenty of things she wasn't ready to discuss with her family just yet, anyway.

"Did you guys have fun?" Maxine asked.

"So much fun," Hunter replied. "I got to see Kaleb Chatterson a bunch and we went kayaking and biking and saw a movie and everything. It was a blast."

"Kaleb Chatterson, huh?" her sister asked Hunter, but Molly knew the question was really directed at her. Luckily, Hunter launched into a dialogue about some video game something or other and Molly took the opportunity to excuse herself and go to the restroom.

She'd been careful about monitoring her blood sugar more often while she'd been babysitting her nephew, administering her doses of insulin prior to every meal. At the theater, she'd calculated the amount of carbs in her popcorn, but then mindlessly shoved a handful of M&Ms in her mouth when Hunter had passed her the box during the movie.

Molly had been mentally kicking herself for the mistake the whole drive here and had even been pushing her rented four-cylinder Toyota to mach speeds to make it back to Sugar Falls just in case she had another episode. She heard the machine beep and let out a sigh of relief at the number. It was a little high, but she was still within the normal range. Knowing that she'd be eating soon, she gave herself another dose.

When she stepped out of the restroom, the scent of garlic and whatever else her brother-in-law was cooking reached her. The kitchen was huge and opened up to a sprawling living room. Cooper somehow managed to look incredibly manly while he bustled around with mixing bowls and pans as Maxine pulled out one of the counter stools next to hers and waved Molly over.

"How was the babymoon?" Molly quickly asked her sister, hoping that if she could keep them talking, she could avoid answering questions about herself. At least, it had worked well enough when Hunter occupied Kaleb with plenty of inquiries throughout breakfast. Mmm. Breakfast. Her stomach rumbled. That had been quite a few hours ago and the popcorn she'd inhaled at the movies wasn't holding her over. She was starving.

"I said, how long is your leave?" Maxine asked, and Molly realized she'd totally tuned her sister out.

The truth was Molly didn't know how long she was staying. Her commanding officer had told her to take some time off and to think about things before making any big decisions about her career. Assuming the Bureau of Personnel told her she would still have one, which was doubtful. "Oh. Maybe a couple of weeks? You know how the military is when it comes to that sort of thing."

"In that case, I'm glad Cooper is making all your favorite foods for dinner tonight. Baked macaroni and cheese, sweet potato casserole, garlic bread and coffee cake with brown sugar crumble."

Uh-oh. Carbs, carbs and more carbs. Molly couldn't eat any of that. At least, she didn't think she could. Did sweet potato casserole count as a vegetable?

"Were you planning to serve any salad with that?" Molly asked, then immediately regretted it when her sister squinted at her suspiciously.

"Not unless your diet has done a complete one-eighty from the last time I've seen you, Moll Doll."

Actually, Molly's entire life had just done a complete one-eighty, along with a few barrel rolls, a pitch-back and quite possibly an upcoming defensive spiral. But she wasn't about to admit that. "Nah, I think I just ate too much popcorn and my stomach has been a little sensitive lately."

She caught her sister giving a pointed look to Cooper.

"I saw that!" Molly said.

"Saw what?"

"That face you made right now at your husband. What's that supposed to mean?"

"It's just that my stomach was sensitive a few months ago," Maxine said, then gave her an encouraging smile. "Back when I was in my first trimester."

Molly gasped. "I'm not pregnant."

"Don't get mad at me for asking. All I know is that you and Trevor called off the wedding and you never said why, and now you're on some sort of extended leave, and I just figured…" Maxine let her voice trail off.

"I'm pretty sure I wouldn't have called off my wedding if I was expecting a child."

"Some people do." Maxine shrugged her shoulders. "So then, why did you guys break up?"

The question threw Molly for a loop. This wasn't the kind of thing her family normally talked about. In fact, when Beau, Maxine's first husband, died in a car crash ten years ago, Molly had no idea that her sister's marriage had been on the rocks until she overheard Kylie and their other friend, Mia, whispering in the restroom at the funeral home.

Molly looked at Cooper, who had his back to them and was chopping lettuce, presumably for an unplanned salad. No doubt, he was attentively listening to their discussion—he was a cop, after all. Fortunately, though, he was polite enough to pretend otherwise.

There were other things she wasn't ready to divulge, but her breakup was the least of her worries. "He was cheating on me."

"With someone else?"

Molly glanced at her brother-in-law, who was holding himself perfectly still. She hoped he was better than his wife when it came to interrogations. "Of course with someone else. That's usually how cheating works."

"Sorry. You're right. Did you confront him?"

"I didn't really have to. He was there when I walked in and…they were…in the middle of…um, a very romantic meal."

"How do you know it was romantic?"

"Because they were feeding each other directly from Chinese takeout containers."

"But didn't he try to explain or anything?"

"They also weren't wearing any clothes at the time." Molly shrugged. "What was there to explain?"

Cooper made a choking sound, but instead of being shocked into minding her own business, Maxine only studied her.

"What?"

"You don't sound very heartbroken."

Crap. Her sister would never buy the excuse that Molly was in Sugar Falls recovering from a failed relationship if she couldn't squeeze out some sort of emotion. But the truth was, she'd hardly given Trevor that much thought lately. In fact, she initially went on her non-honeymoon thinking she would sort some things out and mourn the breakup. However, all she ended up mourning was her formerly healthy, active, career-filled life. Having only gotten her formal diagnosis a few days before she'd caught Trevor, the broken engagement was just a temporary diversion from facing everything else going on in her life. By the end of the vacation, she'd wound up feeling more like she'd just dodged a bullet.

"You know me." Molly lifted her hands up in a careless gesture. "I like to keep my head down and focus on the mission."

"Is the mission to distract yourself with a new guy?" Maxine smirked, then shifted toward the front of her seat when Molly tilted her head to the side. "I know it's none of my business but the word on the street is that you and Kaleb Chatterson were looking pretty chummy on Friday afternoon in Duncan's parking lot."

Molly felt hollow. Her mouth moved, but no words came out.

"Small town," Maxine explained. "And Elaine Marconi said she ran into you guys at the Cowgirl Up Café this morning, which only confirmed all the gossip."

This was it. Molly could come clean and tell her sister about the diabetes and how Kaleb had helped her when she'd needed some insulin the other day and that everything was fine and under control. That's what a normal, courageous person would do. And Molly had always considered herself extremely courageous, if only relatively normal.

Which was why she was surprised when the only explanation she gave was a nervous chuckle.

"I knew it!" Maxine pointed an accusing finger at her. "You and Kaleb Chatterson are a thing. I can't wait to tell Kylie that it's true. Frankly, as far as a rebound relationship goes, you could do a lot worse."

Molly made a noncommittal sound through her tense lips. Cooper had abandoned the lettuce on the cutting board and had his hands linked behind his neck—either to use his forearms to cover his ears or to brace for impact.

"I mean, it *is* only a rebound thing, right?" Maxine asked.

Molly's stomach felt like the empty hull of a bombed-out cargo plane, but she chalked it up to hunger. If this was what it took to get her family off her back, then who was she to throw them off her misguided course?

## Chapter Five

Kaleb was sprawled out on his sister's sectional, stretching out his back and trying to overcome the lingering soreness from that jarring ATV ride this afternoon. His cell phone vibrated in his pocket and he had to wait until his twin nieces created a suitable distraction in their high chairs so that he could pull the thing out and check it without getting another lecture from his dad about today's technology-dependent society.

He didn't recognize the number on his screen, but when he opened the message, he couldn't help the smile that floated to his face. It could only be from one person.

We have a Code Sister in effect. I repeat. A Code Sister.

He typed back a response. What in the world is a Code Sister?

A few dots appeared on his screen, only to vanish just as quickly. Damn. What had Molly been about to say? Did Maxine find out about her diabetes? He typed another question mark and pressed Send. His toes twitched inside his sneakers and his palms itched. He didn't take his eyes off the screen as he sat up straighter. The only time Kaleb got frustrated with technology was when the person on the other end took too long to respond.

But Kylie's loud exclamation of "Oh my gosh!" drew his attention away. "Maxine just texted me and asked if I knew you were dating her sister, Molly."

Kaleb blinked three times. "Dating?"

"Which one is Molly?" Bobby Chatterson, Sr. asked nobody in particular. "Was she at the wedding?"

Kaleb didn't even hear the answer because his pulse was pounding too loudly in his ears. Was this what Molly had meant by a Code Sister? That both of their sisters thought they were dating? *Each other?*

His phone vibrated again as Molly's response appeared. Pretty please just go along with it. I'll owe you.

Something tugged at the corners of his mouth. He doubted Captain Markham used the phrase *pretty please* very often.

"Is it true?" Kylie finally asked him.

"Is what true?"

"Don't try to use the stall tactics on me." Kylie walked over to the couch, one hand firmly planted on her hip, the other waving her electronic tattletale device at his face. "My husband's a psychologist, so I know all those mind tricks."

"If by *dating*, you mean *hanging out*—" Kaleb hated the fact that he'd just used air quotes "—then yes, Molly Markham and I have spent some time together."

That wasn't exactly a lie. He was pretending to be on vacation, anyway, what difference did a pretend girlfriend make at this point? Wait. Was their fake relationship at the girlfriend/boyfriend stage? Molly really should've clarified that. Kaleb desperately avoided those types of conversations with women in his real life. He didn't do commitments, and he certainly didn't discuss them. Usually, when a woman he was dating starting dropping hints about getting more serious, he had Angela email them on his behalf. So then how did one bring that up with a lady who wasn't even programmed into his contact list? He quickly remedied that by typing in her name under the information screen.

"Is it serious?" his mom asked. Lacey Chatterson's soft eyes grew round and hopeful, her fingers clasped together in front of her in a semiprayerful state.

"Mom!" Kaleb rolled his eyes. "We met for the first time on Friday."

"That doesn't mean anything," his dad said, bringing a bowl of chips to the coffee table. Great, his family was now cornering him on the living room sofa. "Kylie and Drew only knew each other for all of five hours before *they* got married."

"Dad!" His sister followed with a bowl of salsa. Man, they were really settling in for this interrogation. "Drew and I had special circumstances."

It was no secret that his baby sister and her strait-laced husband had gotten drunk in Reno and accidentally ended up at a wedding chapel. But Kaleb didn't believe in accidents. He liked having a plan and sticking to it. Unfortunately, with his family hovering around him, he couldn't exactly text Molly back and ask her what the damn plan was.

Kaleb's company had developed some of the best role-playing games on the market, but those usually involved alternate universes with alien pirates and zombie dragons. Normally, he was good at games as long as he knew the rules. Unfortunately, someone had suddenly thrown him into the role of boyfriend—and unlike the online versions he'd created, this one might actually affect real lives.

"I'm sending Maxine a text inviting her family for dinner on Wednesday," Kylie said as she typed furiously on her phone.

"Wait." Kaleb held up his palm. "I think everyone is getting way too ahead of themselves here."

"Too late." His sister grinned and held up her display screen. "Maxine already accepted."

"Don't you think that's going to be awkward?" Kaleb had been looking down at his own phone so long he had to push his glasses back into place.

"Trust me." Kylie reached out and squeezed his left shoulder. "It's much better to get all this relationship stuff out in the open."

"Listen to your sister, son." His dad squeezed his other shoulder. "She of all people knows what she's talking about."

"Dad!" Kylie gripped the left one tighter, thereby pulling him away from their father. Bobby Chatterson yanked back.

"This is what I mean by awkward." Kaleb dislodged himself from their not-so-reassuring grips and stood up. "Our family always gets so competitive and loud and chaotic and you guys are going to end up scaring her away."

His sister's inspecting scan moved from his messy

hair down to his feet and back up again. "The only thing that's going to scare Molly away is that outfit."

"What's wrong with my clothes?" Kaleb asked, holding out the hem of his T-shirt so he could see what design was on it. He loved his collection of quirky T-shirts.

"Nothing, if you're a fifteen-year-old boy," Kylie replied.

"No fifteen-year-old boy of mine would wear sneakers that cost as much as those." His dad pointed to Kaleb's custom-made designer shoes. "Are those supposed to be suede?"

"Perhaps you have something a little more impressive?" his mom asked. "What do you normally wear to meetings?"

"I normally wear this to meetings." Kaleb crossed his arms in front of his chest. "I don't exactly have a suit-and-tie kind of job."

Actually, he did have a couple of well-tailored suits back at his penthouse. In Seattle. Where he wasn't on vacation. Yet, even if he had access to all the best clothes in the world, he still wouldn't wear them. It was one thing to pretend to be dating a woman he'd barely met. It was another to pretend to be something he wasn't.

Which brought him back to why he didn't do relationships in the first place. People, especially the pretty female variety, always wanted to believe that he was some sort of superstar—some sort of megapowerful billionaire who was in the market for a trophy wife. In reality, all he wanted was a simple life where he could be left alone to concentrate on his work. Unfortunately, the women who tended to throw themselves at him weren't interested in the boring, geeky version of Kaleb Chatterson. In the end, they ended up wasting their time when they found out he wasn't going to change.

His phone finally vibrated again.

"Is that her?" His sister jumped up from the couch, trying to read the display. He put his hand on her forehead, holding her at a distance the way he'd done when they were kids and she'd wanted one of his collector's edition action figures for her Barbie Dreamhouse.

He had to read the screen quickly because Kylie's kicking range had apparently gotten longer since she was seven years old. It also seemed as though all the splits and cheerleading jumps from her college years had perfected her toe points.

Don't worry about dinner happening on Wednesday. I'll try and tell my sister everything by then.

He'd barely gotten the phone safely tucked into his pocket when he wrapped Kylie into a fierce bear hug. She pinched his ribs before finally hugging him back.

"We're only nosy because we care about you," she mumbled into his shoulder.

"That explains the nosy part, but not the embarrassing part," Kaleb replied, patting her on the head.

"Embarrassing? I promise to be on my best behavior." Kylie stepped out of his arms, her right hand raised as if she were swearing an oath. "But I can't speak for Dad or the rest of our siblings."

Kaleb groaned. While he'd dated his fair share of women, he'd never brought a girlfriend home—pretend or otherwise. If teasing was an Olympic sport, his brothers would win the gold medals, with Kylie tying their old man for the silver. Hopefully, Molly would come clean and tell her sister the truth by then. It would be way less painful for everyone. Or at least for him.

Did you tell her yet?

Kaleb's text was in Molly's in-box when she woke up on Tuesday morning. The digital clock on her screen was still set to military time and she tried not to deliver bad news to anyone if the word *oh* was part of the hour. Then she realized he must've been talking about last night. She hoped he wasn't as mortified about hearing the lie as she had been telling it. Although, really, it wasn't so much a lie as a diversionary tactic. It was unfortunate that Kaleb was caught in the crosshairs, but he was the one who'd put his reputation in harm's way. Twice, she might add.

I tried to, Molly wrote back. Then added, Couldn't find the right time.

It was the truth. If Maxine would've asked her about her job again, Molly would've probably said something. Or if her sister had made a comment about her not eating all her favorite foods—and, oh, man, had that been a challenge when she'd shoved mouthful after mouthful of salad into her mouth and then claimed to be too full for more than a small bite of anything else—she might have mentioned it. But their family didn't get all up in each other's business like that. They certainly didn't talk about personal things. In fact, that whole conversation about Trevor cheating on her was more than enough failure to share in one night.

Molly would like to think that it was a matter of respecting boundaries. So if Maxine wasn't going to pry, then Molly didn't want to burden her with any unnecessary knowledge.

But maybe the Chatterson family wasn't like that.

Her phone chimed again and she looked at the image Kaleb had just sent her. It was a cartoon elephant up in a tree, balancing its huge, cowering body on a tiny branch with a tiny mouse below.

She replied with a picture of what looked to be a honeycomb.

What is that?

Beeswax, she typed. Then added, So that you can mind your own.

She pulled the soft, expensive sheets over her head. At least she had her sister's apartment to herself today. She could spend the day researching healthy meal options and forming a plan to tell her sister the truth.

A motorcycle engine revved outside her window.

Or she could do one of those ATV tour things that Kaleb had mentioned yesterday. She'd been beyond jealous when he'd brought it up. While it wasn't a plane, with a powerful motor, some off-course trails and the wind in her hair, it could be the next best thing. Molly did her clearest thinking when she was piloting something.

She sat up in bed and placed a call. But the company who did the tours had a group from the senior center scheduled for that morning and Molly didn't want to get stuck going the speed recommended by the AARP. In fact, she didn't want to go with anyone at all. Not even a guide. She assured the man who answered the phone at Russell Sports that she knew what she was doing and only required the rental. It would also be cheaper that way.

Surveying Maxine's cupboards, she found a questionable-looking granola bar and pulled a couple of bottles of water from the fridge. She threw those and her insulin kit into a canvas cinch sack she could sling onto her back during the ride. Then she questioned whether she should pack something else. She didn't want to go to Duncan's and risk running into another gossiping biddy. However, she also didn't want to get stuck out on some wilderness trail with only one healthy snack.

In the end, Molly stopped off at Domino's Deli in town and grabbed a turkey sub on a whole-wheat roll and a bag of pretzels, which looked like the least caloric option on the potato chip rack. What else did she need? It was more food than she would've taken on a twenty-four-hour combat training exercise. Even Kaleb would've been proud of her foresight.

Nope. She refused to think about him and what he would think. Today was for her. Molly would deal with her sister and Kaleb and everyone else tonight.

Unfortunately, by the time she'd made it back to the apartment that evening, she was covered in mud and so jacked up on adrenaline the only thing she wanted to confront was a hot shower and the last half of *Pearl Harbor* on the movie channel.

On Wednesday morning, Molly awoke to another text from Kaleb.

We're grilling chicken tonight, but I don't know what the sides will be. I'll let you know as soon as I can, but make sure you check your levels before you get here. Maybe bring a snack just in case.

Molly almost threw the phone across the room. She didn't know what annoyed her more. The fact that he was bossing her about food choices again or his assumption that she still hadn't talked to Maxine.

It didn't help her mood that the sweet vanilla scent of the cookies baking downstairs had permeated the apartment. And she couldn't have any. Probably ever again. Ugh. She needed coffee.

She sat up in bed and checked her blood levels, giving herself a morning dose of the longer lasting insulin. Then she weaved her way to the kitchen in nothing but her dingy gray Air Force Academy T-shirt and a loose pair of running shorts she had to roll up at the waist to stay on her hips. Turning on the coffeemaker, she caught her reflection in the microwave glass and yanked on her rubber band to adjust her sloppy ponytail from the side of her head to more of a forty-five-degree angle.

Molly had just set a fresh K-Cup to brew when a knock sounded at the door. She figured it had to be Maxine taking a break from the shop downstairs and sighed. They might as well get this talk over with.

When she swung open the door, Molly wasn't braced for the shock of seeing Kaleb on the small landing, holding a brown bag from Duncan's Market.

Molly looked past him, down the stairs toward the bakery below. He followed her gaze and—without her asking the question on the tip of her sleepy tongue—he said, "Yes, your sister is down there, and yes, she saw me come up."

Her caffeine-deprived brain was still a little fuzzy, so

she scratched at her head, then froze, realizing how her hair must look. She crossed her arms, then uncrossed them to tug the hem of her shorts down so it wouldn't look like she wasn't wearing anything below, before crossing her arms again. "What are you doing here?"

"Now, now. Is that any way to greet the man you're dating?"

Her reflexes shot to life and she whispered, "Get in here," before snatching the front of his T-shirt and yanking him inside.

The problem came when she didn't sidestep quickly enough and the solid muscular wall of Kaleb's chest crashed into her, forcing him to wrap an arm around her to steady them both. The cotton of his shirt was soft and worn under her fingers, and when she took a steadying breath, she inhaled the lemon and cedar scent of his soap.

He wiggled his eyebrows and said, "This greeting's more like it."

"Huh?" His hand slid lower until it cupped the rounding curve just below her waistband and her palms instinctively moved up over his pecs toward his wide shoulders.

"Definitely more like the kind of reception I would expect from my girlfriend."

Girlfriend? He had a girlfriend? His heavily lidded eyes were staring intently at her lips and it suddenly dawned on Molly that he meant her. She banged her big toe into the hardwood floor as she hopped backward.

"Don't worry." She held her palms up. "I'm going to tell Maxine this morning so we don't have to do that whole dating charade thing tonight."

"Too late," he said, then strode past her and set the bag on a kitchen counter.

"What do you mean, too late?" She tried to get her breathing under control as he pulled groceries out. "And what are you doing?"

He held up a carton of eggs. "I'm fixing you breakfast. What does it look like I'm doing?"

That didn't explain anything at all. But she certainly wasn't going to turn down a free meal. "Did I miss something?"

"Yeah. You missed your opportunity to tell your sister the truth."

"Dinner isn't until six." She looked at the clock on the microwave. "I have all day to tell her."

He propped up an electronic tablet on some sort of holder and began tapping the screen. "Not anymore, you…" He was so intent on whatever he was doing he didn't finish his sentence.

Molly waved a hand in front of his face. His only response was to sigh and look up at her.

"What's going on?" she asked.

"I had my assistant, Angela, send me a video on how to make an omelet and the Wi-Fi at Duncan's was spotty this morning so I need to watch it again to make sure I bought all the right ingredients."

"Kaleb!" Molly had to restrain herself from banging her head against the cabinet in frustration. "I meant what is going with us?"

"Sorry, I thought we had the kind of fake relationship where we don't explain things to each other."

She closed her eyes and counted to five. When she opened them, he had his hands on his hips, one brow raised as if he needed to ensure her full attention. "I guess I deserve that. But I said I was going to talk to Maxine and come clean. I would've texted you the all clear afterward."

"And I said it was too late."

"But you didn't say why."

"Because I had to spend the entire day yesterday trapped on a white-water raft with all of my family, answering questions about you. Questions I didn't necessarily know the answers to, but had to make stuff up as I went along so that I could keep your secret safe."

"I'm really sorry about that." She tried to make an apologetic face. "But at least you got to go white-water rafting."

"Molly," he growled, then pinched the bridge of his nose. "Aren't you paying attention?"

She nodded, then slowly shook her head. "But I'm trying to."

"My family now thinks we're dating. On Monday night I simply didn't correct them. But yesterday I actively engaged in, well, I hate to use the word *deception*, but it's the only thing that fits."

"Oh."

"Then, this morning, my mom told me that my eyes lit up whenever I talked about you and that she was so glad I'd finally met someone I was interested in because she worries about me working too much."

A tingling of warmth started in her toes and spread up to her torso. "Your eyes lit up when you talked about me?"

His neck turned a charming shade of pink as the muscles near his jaw line pulled tighter. "No, it was probably only the river water. I had my contacts in. Anyway, my point is that my family now thinks there's something between us and I've never lied to them before."

"But we're not dating."

"We are now. This—" he gestured to the groceries on the counter "—is a breakfast date. I'm told that women think it's very romantic when men cook for them."

"But you didn't ask me."

"Did you ask me when you told Maxine we were dating?"

"I didn't tell her! She assumed."

"However, you didn't correct her."

"You didn't correct your family, either."

"Which is why I'm not going to make liars out of us." He smiled in triumph, as if he'd just masterminded some great escape.

"I don't get it. Are we or are we not pretending we're dating?"

"We're not pretending anything. We don't have to. You're not in town long, I'm not in town long. We'll go on a few dates—in a strictly platonic sense—and then, when we leave Sugar Falls, we say goodbye."

"We do?"

"Yes." He began cracking eggs into a bowl. "You hate long-distance relationships."

"I also hate being told what to do. Even by someone who is strictly platonic."

"Well, too bad." He unlocked his phone and pulled up her text messages. "You said it yourself. You owe me."

She took a gulp of coffee, but without the half-and-half to cool it down, it burned her tongue. "I know what I said."

His tablet, phone and smartwatch all chimed simultaneously. "I forgot I have a video chat in half an hour."

"You're going to take a conference call over here?" She smirked, her eyes narrowing. Kaleb acted like he was the one doing her the favor, but she bet the real reason he came over here was to get some work done without his family bothering him. "While we're on a date, Cupcake?"

"Cupcake?"

"Isn't that what we call each other?"

"No. We call each other by our names. Because we're grown-ups."

"Well, I'm going to go take a shower, Cupcake. Let me know when my omelet's ready."

## Chapter Six

That evening, Kaleb stared at his reflection in the bathroom mirror at his sister's house. Molly and her family
would be here in less than an hour and Kylie's words
about his taste in clothing were coming back to haunt
him. Not that he was trying to impress anyone, but when
Molly had answered the door this morning in her T-shirt
and short shorts, Kaleb had been tempted to kiss her right
there on the spot. Then she'd pulled him toward her and
it was all he could do to remind himself that this whole
dating plan they'd come up with wasn't supposed to be
serious.

Speaking of which, their official first date this morning hadn't gone exactly according to plan. Well, the
omelet part did at least. He'd no more than plated the
vegetable-filled eggs when Molly'd come out of the
bathroom wearing athletic leggings and a sweatshirt

so loose the oversize neck draped to the side, leaving a tan shoulder bare. Well, bare except for the pink bikini strap tied behind her damp, wavy ponytail.

She smelled like the coconut-mango smoothies he used to get when he was a kid vacationing in Hawaii for real with his family, as opposed to the forced kind they now endured as adults. Kaleb had been tempted to draw her in closer to see if her skin tasted as good as it smelled. Instead, he'd doused the flames of attraction by handing her a plate and a stack of papers he'd printed out that morning.

"I thought you could look over these while I'm on my conference chat," he'd said. She rolled her eyes as he set up his laptop on one end of the table, and at some point between his conference call with his lawyers in the Tokyo office over the Japanese production rights to his latest game and his brainstorming session with his writing staff about the possibility of giving one of his video characters their own cartoon show, Molly had taken off.

He'd been wearing his headset and pacing back and forth in the small living room when she'd given him a discreet wave, pointed toward the stairs and made a gesture with her two fingers indicating she was going downstairs. He'd assumed she was going to hang out with her sister, but after an hour, he'd discovered she'd left him a note on the back of the diabetic menu plan Angela had emailed him this morning.

Thanks for the "date." And for bringing up white-water rafting. I'm going to spend the day on the river. M.

In the past, when a woman he was dating was annoyed that he wasn't paying her enough attention, she pouted or started a fight. However, Molly hadn't looked the least bit annoyed. Actually, when she'd left, she'd looked pretty carefree and a little relieved. Just to be sure, he'd sent her a text apologizing for being occupied with his business calls, and she'd replied with a thumbs-up emoji. Clearly, neither one of them were expecting candlelight and roses out of this relationship.

So then why was he standing here in his sister's bathroom suddenly concerned with his appearance? It wasn't like he was back in high school, wearing pimple cream and his back brace under a *Battlestar Galactica* T-shirt?

The doorbell sounded over the barking of his brother Bobby Junior's six-month-old goldendoodle and his five nieces and nephews. Or was it seven now? Did Kylie's brother-in-law's kids count as honorary Chattersons? Kaleb braced his hands against the counter and reminded himself that no matter how good Molly might look out there, they were only dating—in a strictly platonic sense—for eight more days.

Besides, she was probably more worried about whether he'd slip and bring up her diabetes than whether he was wearing some fancy collared shirt.

What was he so worried about, anyway? Kaleb was a global leader in a multi-billion-dollar industry. Surely, he could handle one crazy family dinner.

He ran a hand through his hair, then made his way toward the living room, dodging a Nerf football, shaking off a puppy sniffing his pant leg as if it was about to mark its territory and stepping over his twin nieces working on something called "tummy time." Through the cluster of men standing in the corner discussing the best bull pens in the major leagues, he caught a view of the open kitchen where Molly was thanking his father for the plastic cup the older man just handed her. Knowing that whatever frozen concoction his dad was serving was most likely on her discarded list of high sugar foods to avoid, he sprang into action.

"Hey, you," Kaleb said when he put an arm around Molly's shoulder, somewhat out of breath after the obstacle course of kids and pets he'd had to wade through to get to her. His approach must've lacked the finesse he'd intended because her body jerked back just enough to slosh the fruity liquid around in her cup.

She frowned in response.

"Oh, great. Strawberry daiquiris. My favorite," he exclaimed, prying the beverage from her hand and taking a huge gulp before whispering in her ear, "You're not supposed to drink stuff like this."

"And you're supposed to be my fake date, not my endocrinologist," she whispered back.

"Not fake," he mumbled, then took another sip. "Platonic."

"So, Molly," Kylie interrupted them, her eyes sharp and focused as though she was ready to pounce on the merest hint of tension between them. "I know you've already met Kaleb, the black sheep of our family. But let me introduce you to the rest of the Chatterson clan."

And so it began. Kaleb would try to make things go as smoothly as possible, but when it came to his loud, opinionated family, he knew better than to make any promises he couldn't keep.

"Maxine ran through your family tree on the car ride over here, so I think I've got all the adults' names," Molly said to Kaleb as they stood on the deck overlooking the lake, her initial jitters of meeting everyone tamped down now that she knew the only nerve-racking part would be to get through the rest of the evening without blowing their cover. "But I can't remember which kids go with which parents."

Most of the men were gathered around the grill, which had been moved to the grassy area below. Maxine was sitting with her swollen ankles propped up on another seat, the ladies clustered nearby drinking their strawberry daiquiris while Hunter and the rest of the kids played some sort of made-up game that resembled Wiffle ball. Or badminton. Or a combination of both. Molly wondered if they were even following a set of rules.

"So the twin girls in that playpen thing belong to Kylie and her husband, Drew." Kaleb used his beer bottle to point. "Those three redheads chasing after the dog who just stole the pink ball belong to my brother Bobby Junior. His wife is off at some health spa this week, which is fine because she hates our family vacations and isn't afraid to let everyone know."

"How could anyone hate this?" Molly asked. It was true; so far everyone had been so nice and some of the stories they'd told about Kaleb were not only hilarious, they also took the attention off her. They were nothing like her family. Sure, they teased each other mercilessly, but each sibling gave as good as they got. Nobody was spared and no secret was safe. The Chattersons were open and warm and playful and, within thirty minutes, made Molly feel more relaxed and at ease than she'd been during the past few weeks.

"Are you kidding? It's a circus, but with more prodding of the caged animals and a few extra clowns who aren't very funny."

"I think you secretly love it," she said, then laughed when he rolled his eyes. "You've only looked at your smartwatch five times and haven't called your assistant once. Clearly, you're not that bored."

"Not bored? I'm on high alert. I can't let my guard down for a second around these jokesters. You know what these big families are like."

"Actually," she said, then cleared her throat when a hint of emotion welled up in her chest, "I don't. I mean, there's a lot of us, but we're not exactly the type of family that vacations together."

"Um, aren't you vacationing with your sister right now?" Kaleb asked.

Molly schooled her expression so that she didn't appear too uneasy. "This isn't exactly a vacation."

"What do you mean?"

"It's more of a temporary medical leave. I don't know when I'll be going back to work." She refused to make eye contact with him, not wanting to see the concern she knew would be reflected there. But because she'd already admitted as much, she added, "If I return to work at all."

"I'm guessing you're not going to tell your sister about that, either?"

"Eventually. Maybe." So much for that short-lived feeling of relaxation. When he kept looking at her, she felt the need to explain. "People always assumed that because we're sisters we're born confidantes. I mean, don't get me wrong. It isn't like we fight or dislike each other. But growing up in the Markham household, there was a pretty high value placed on privacy. Especially when you were number five out of six. By the time I came along, everyone had already been forced to share rooms, toys and even their ice-cream bowls. Anyway, nobody wanted to have to share their dreams or their innermost feelings, either. At least, not with their kid sister. On the rare occasions when we did have family dinners, silence was certainly golden. My siblings definitely aren't as informative and entertaining as yours. You're very lucky, Kaleb."

He studied her in the fading sunlight and she rocked back on her sandaled heels. Was he going to kiss her? Did she want him to? Desire curled around her tummy. A part of her had craved his lips on hers since the first time she saw him. But she certainly didn't want him making a move only because he felt sorry for her.

To get his attention—and hers—off a possible very public display of affection, she went back to their original conversation. "And those two boys, the other set of twins, who do they belong to?"

"Those little rascals aren't technically Chattersons. But they might as well be. And between me and you, they might be my favorite kids ever. Their parents are Carmen and Luke. Luke is Drew's twin brother."

"That makes three sets? Wow!"

"Yep. Moving on, the overweight basset hound belongs to Kane and Julia. And my brother Kevin over there—" he pointed to the guy wearing a ball cap and sunglasses, nursing a hangover on a lounge chair "—he can't even take care of a houseplant, let alone another living thing."

"Hey, Molly," one of the twin boys yelled up to them. "You ready for another drink? Uncle Kevin pays us five dollars every time we bring him a beer."

Before she could politely decline, Kaleb announced to the entire family below, "She's had enough."

Molly felt her face turn as red as the melted liquid in her red plastic cup.

"You don't have to make me sound like a lush who needs to be cut off." Then, to prove to his family that Kaleb wasn't calling the shots, she said, "I'll have one more, but I only have two dollars."

"You're on," the boy said, hustling over to the bar before his stepmom, who was still on duty and dressed in her police uniform, slapped a hand to her forehead and followed behind.

"I really don't think that's a good idea," Kaleb said, close on Molly's heels as she descended the steps. "There's a ton of sugar in those things and you don't want to…you know…with everyone watching."

"I also don't want to stand out or have your family think that there's something wrong with me," she replied through a tight smile. "I won't actually drink it."

He maneuvered himself in front of her path and quickly turned to face her, forcing her to stop one step above him. Their eyes were on the same level. "How about a Diet Coke instead?"

"How about I act like a normal houseguest and take an extra dose of insulin later?" She tried to step around him, but his hands reached out to grasp her hips and another one of those currents of electricity shot through her. Yet she didn't know if this was from desire or anger.

"Hey, look," the other twin called out. "Uncle Kaleb is gonna kiss her!"

If she hadn't already been blushing to the roots of her hair, she certainly was now. "You weren't going to kiss me, were you?"

"I didn't intend to, but now that everyone is watching us, it'll look weird if I don't. Unless you don't want me to…"

"Kiss her, Uncle Kaleb!" a little redhead girl yelled.

Molly's eyes widened, hoping he'd give her some sort of direction on how to handle this situation. When Kaleb placed a chaste kiss on her forehead, Kevin led all the kids in a round of disappointing boos.

"That was the best you could do?" Molly whispered before Carmen handed her the strawberry daiquiri and waved away the two dollars. She took a slug of the drink, hoping to cool her cheeks down, then quickly handed it over to Kaleb when the sugary contents hit her throat. Whew. She was going to pay for that later.

"I assure you, I could do a lot better," Kaleb said quietly, his thumb making slow circles along her hip.

Looking at the heat in his eyes, Molly didn't doubt for a second that if they didn't have a captive audience, the man would more than prove himself right.

The following morning, Kaleb told himself that he was only going to the Cowgirl Up Café for breakfast because he'd been craving some biscuits and gravy and he wanted to escape Bobby Junior's three noisy kids, who had overflowed from Kylie's lakefront house and were now intruding on his solitary stay at Kane's place. Not because he was hoping to see Molly in town. And definitely not because he was still looking for the opportunity to get her alone and make good on his promise of a more thorough kiss.

He parked the truck on Snowflake Boulevard and as he passed two horses—he did a double take to see that the animals were real and not just some sort of small-town stage prop—tied to a post outside the restaurant, the aroma of bacon and coffee almost made him forget the teasing his brothers had put him through after Molly had left last night. Almost.

When he pulled open the saloon-style front door of the café, his relief at seeing her sitting in a back booth upholstered with cow print was short-lived. Because sitting across the table from her was Kylie and Mia, a friend of his sister's and Maxine's from college.

There was a row of empty seats at the counter, but there was no way Kaleb could get away without acknowledging his sister, her friend and the woman he was supposedly dating. He dropped his laptop bag on one of the chairs at the counter, claiming his space in a way to announce to everyone that he had no intention of joining the women. He'd go say hello quickly, then come back over here to go through several financial reports and send out a few emails before his father started calling around looking for him.

"Ladies," he said by way of greeting, right before he spotted the half-eaten cinnamon roll in front of Molly. "What's going on?"

Really, he was asking Molly about her food choices, but thankfully Kylie thought the world revolved around her and assumed he was speaking to all of them.

"We're planning a baby shower for Maxine," Kylie said. "You remember my friend Mia, right?"

"Of course." Kaleb reached across to shake the petite brunette's hand. "Nice to see you again."

His sister and Mia went on to tell him about when they were having the party, but his eyes were drawn back to the pastry Molly had no doubt been eating before he'd arrived. Their talk of baby bottles and finger foods and stork decorations distracted him from what he really wanted to do, which was scope out Molly for any evidence of symptoms that might suggest she was about to have another one of her episodes.

However, Molly's expression was suspiciously riveted on whatever the other women were saying and she'd barely acknowledged his presence. She was so busted.

"Well, it sounds like you guys have things under control, so if you'll excuse me—" Kaleb nodded toward his laptop bag on the counter stool "—I'm going to have a quick bite before Dad calls me with whatever plans are on today's Chatterson family agenda."

"It's Jet Skiing," Kylie said. "Drew and Kane were pulling the Sea-Doos out of the boat shed when I left, and if they find out you're over here on that stupid computer again while they're taking orders from Dad, you're going to be put in charge of filling up all the water balloons for the Aqua Battle this afternoon."

"Nobody likes a rat, Kylie." Kaleb winked at his sister before turning to Molly. "Since you're not going to eat this, I'll finish it for you."

He snatched the cinnamon roll from the table just as she was reaching for the plate. The heat of her glare penetrated his back as he returned to his seat, but he didn't care. She would be thanking him later. He opened up his computer as an older waitress with hair much bigger and more peach colored than nature had intended leaned a spandex-covered hip against the counter. He recognized Freckles, the owner of the restaurant, from his last visit to town.

"It's been two years since you had one of my famous cinnamon rolls, Kaleb Chatterson," she said as she pulled a pencil from behind an earlobe lined with studded earrings. "You know I'd give you your own. You don't have to go around stealing them from my pretty customers. Even if you *are* dating her."

Kaleb risked a peek at the woman in question, praying she didn't hear what the sassy waitress had just announced. But the older woman snorted. "Small-town rumor mills been around long before you fancy computer kids ever invented that social media nonsense."

"Technically, Freckles," Kaleb defended himself, "I had one when I was in here on Monday."

"No, you had the cinnamon roll French toast. Two different things." Freckles used the pencil to gesture toward Monica, who'd waited on them a few days ago. "Darlin, even on my days off, I know what people are eating in my own restaurant. And more important, I know who they're eating it with."

The woman's wink revealed a smudge of green eye shadow that didn't match the fuchsia lipstick on her smirking grin. Kaleb didn't mind the good-natured teasing, especially since it kept her from noticing the way Molly had just downed two glasses of ice water and was beating a fast retreat to the restrooms.

"Well, today, I'll be having the biscuits and gravy and I'll be eating it alone," Kaleb said, not bothering to look at the menu.

When Freckles turned toward the kitchen, Kaleb waited a full forty-five seconds before following Molly to the back of the restaurant. Thankfully, the bathrooms were down the hall and none of the diners could see him as he waited outside. After a few minutes, or maybe only one—who was counting—he knocked on the door to the ladies' room. There was no answer so he jiggled the handle. It was unlocked, and he knew that if it was anything like the men's, there was only one separate stall inside.

He weighed his choices briefly before a vision of Molly, pale and nearly passed out as she had been inside Duncan's Market that day they'd first met, replayed in his mind.

He opened the door and was only slightly relieved that he hadn't walked in on another woman. He recognized her green sneakers under the stall. "Molly, is that you?"

She gasped. "Who else would it be?"

"Are you okay?"

"Kaleb, do you know this is a ladies' room?"

"If I didn't before, the hot-pink cowboy hat wallpaper would've given it away."

The sound of a plastic lid being snapped shut, followed by a zipper came from inside the stall before she finally emerged, shoving her little black case into her tote bag. "What are you doing in here?"

He nodded toward the straw purse. "What was your number?"

"My number is *supposed* to be that I don't have a stupid number. Two months ago, nobody cared about my levels. I didn't even know I *had* levels. Yet, now I'm living in this completely foreign land with a whole new language I never knew existed and every few hours, a drop of blood on a little test strip is supposed to tell me what kind of day I'm having."

"But you're not alone. People are going through exact same thing you are and—"

"Where, Kaleb?" Molly cut him off. "Where are these people who are going through this? Because they aren't here in the ladies' room with me. And they certainly aren't in my squadron, which is where I belong. I know that other people have this same disease. I even know that they have support groups. But right now, I'm still grieving my former life—the life that I probably will never get to go back to—and I don't need anyone else scrutinizing my every move and constantly reminding me of what I've lost."

His throat constricted and he wanted to argue that she hadn't lost everything. He'd downloaded several books on diabetes to his iPad and was convinced that she could manage it if given the right support tools. However, he also knew that she needed to grieve in her own way and come to these conclusions on her own. At least, that's what some of the experts said.

However, he couldn't stand by and let her hide her head in the sand on the deserted island she'd created for herself. "You're right that I'm not going through this, and I can't begin to imagine how I would react if I was. But you can't get mad at me for caring about you."

"I don't *need* you to care about me." She sighed but her lips weren't pressed into the rigid line of annoyance she usually made whenever he told her something she didn't want to hear. He hated seeing her defeated and had a feeling that she would respond better to being pestered than to being pitied.

"Well, too bad. I care about all the women I rescue from grocery stores." The barest hint of a smile quirked her lips. "Now, do you want to tell me what your level was or do I need to need to wrestle that glucose meter away from you and read it for myself?"

"Wrestle?" A spark suddenly flashed in her eyes and he knew the anger route had been the way to go. "I may not be as big and muscular as you, Kaleb Chatterson, but I've been trained in hand-to-hand combat and there's no way I'd go down without a fight."

"Is that a challenge?" he asked, taking a step closer to her.

Her eyes narrowed, her nostrils flared ever so slightly and he knew she was thinking of what would happen if both of their bodies came into that type of physical proximity. Because that was the exact thing he was thinking.

He moved closer.

"One fifty-eight," she said in a rush. "A little high, but I got my insulin quickly enough, so I'm fine."

He let out a deep breath toward the ceiling. "Good thing you didn't eat that entire cinnamon roll."

"You mean before you stole it from me?" She put her hands on her hips.

Yep, putting her on the defensive was the best way to get her to respond. The problem was, with the slight hitch in her breathing and the way she was looking at him, his body was beginning to respond, as well.

And he did still owe her a kiss. In fact, her pouting lips looked soft and full and pink and even more inviting than they had last night.

He told himself not to do it. But when he took another step toward her, her chin lifted.

He told himself that this would be a mistake. But when he cupped her cheek, her eyelids lowered.

He told himself that after he had one taste, there would be no going back. But when he grazed his lips against hers, she sighed.

He didn't tell himself anything after that.

## Chapter Seven

Kaleb's mouth was warm and welcoming and so very persuasive. One minute, Molly'd been in the bathroom stall, angry at herself for being weak and eating the wrong foods, feeling overwhelmed and like a failure. The next minute, Kaleb was there letting her know that her body was still very much alive.

Molly lifted up onto her tiptoes to wrap her arms fully around his neck, pulling his chest against hers. She didn't know if he'd deepened the kiss or if she did, but their tongues were stroking, exploring and staking claim. He'd been right last night. He definitely could deliver a better kiss.

Still, Molly wanted more. His arousal pressed against her lower belly and she needed to feel that throbbing hardness somewhere else. She hooked a leg around the back of his thigh, tilting her hips upward. Kaleb groaned before sliding his hands under the legs of her running shorts, cupping her bottom in his palms and lifting her up against the wall. She wrapped her calves around his waist, moaning into his mouth as he pressed himself between her open thighs.

She heard an automated whirring sound each time his hips rocked inside of hers, but dismissed it as one of his annoying smart devices. If Kaleb was too focused to worry about his electronics or his company, then who was she to distract him from his mission?

And, oh, what a mission it was. As his lips trailed down her neck, her breathing became labored and she arched her head back, giving him better access while sucking in more air. She slid her fingers through his dark hair, pulling his mouth back to hers right as a cool rush of air came from the doorway.

The open doorway.

"I know it's a small town, but we *do* have hotels here in Sugar Falls," Freckles said before letting out a quiet—thankfully—giggle and slapping her thigh. In Molly's scramble to put her feet down, her knee moved under the sensor of the paper towel machine, and all three sets of eyes followed the trail from the roll inside to the pile folded upon itself on the floor. Freckles giggled again before pulling the door closed behind her.

Left alone with their embarrassment, Molly's choices were to face Kaleb or look at her reflection in the mirror above the sink. She chose the less judgmental of the two options and watched him use the hem of his T-shirt to clean the fog off his glasses. A little bubble of satisfaction floated inside her at the realization that she'd been partially responsible for making him get that steamy. But that bubble was soon skewered through by a sharp needle of returning desire when she saw the tight muscles of his abdomen revealed.

"Here." She tore off the thirty dangling feet of paper towel and held the upper part out to him. His eyes were even bluer without the thick, trendy black frames and she wished she was in a cockpit with an ejection seat so that she could better escape this situation.

"Sorry about that," Kaleb said as he replaced his glasses and bent to retrieve the rest of the towel to stuff into the giant cowboy-boot-shaped garbage can.

"Sorry that you kissed me or sorry that we got busted like that?" Molly asked.

"Actually, I was sorry that we accidentally set off that machine and wasted all that paper. I'm not the least bit sorry that I kissed you. And it certainly doesn't bother me that we got caught."

Of course it wouldn't bother him. It played right into his big dating plan, making everything seem more realistic. Molly tugged on the edges of her running shorts, ensuring they were back in place. But that was a mistake since it drew his gaze to her thighs, causing her muscles underneath to clench as a shudder made its way to her center. If Kaleb kept looking at her like that, they would end up finishing what they started right here in the ladies' room of the Cowgirl Up.

"Kylie and Mia are probably wondering what's taking me so long," she said, then gasped. "Wait, did they see you come in here?"

"I hope not, but to be honest, I was worried that you were getting sick and needed me, and wasn't really paying attention to them."

"Well, we can't very well go back out there together," Molly said. "One of us should stay here."

"You go on ahead. I need a little more time to, uh, get myself under control."

As she retrieved her tote bag from where she must've dropped it on the floor, a flush of warmth rushed up her neck. As she rushed toward the door, the buzz of the paper towel machine was activated again and the sound mocked her all the way out into the hallway.

Mia had already left by the time Molly made it back to the table and Kylie was paying the check. "Are you feeling okay?" Kylie looked up from the credit card receipt she'd been signing, concern evident on her face.

"Fine." Molly forced a smile, not trusting herself to say more to the sister of the man who'd almost taken her against the wall of a public restroom.

"Have you seen Kaleb? I hope he didn't slip out without saying goodbye." The woman didn't look suspicious, but Molly wasn't going to risk further questioning by admitting anything.

"I heard him talking to his assistant on the phone in the men's room."

"Doesn't it drive you crazy that he's always in work mode and can never just relax and let someone else run things for a change? I can't even imagine what he must be like on dates."

"I, uh, we're not really..." They weren't really what? Dating? At least, not seriously. What could Molly say without making it sound like she didn't mind being ignored by a guy who was supposed to be interested in her? "We're not exactly on a date right now. And his business is pretty important."

"His business is successful, not important. The world doesn't need another video game. If that guy thinks he's too busy to... There you are, Brainiac," Kylie said to

Kaleb as he approached the table. "Dad thinks we need to rent a couple more Jet Skis and he's looking for you because they need someone else to drive them over to our house from the rental place."

Jet Skis? Seriously? Why did the Chattersons get to do all the fun, high-speed activities?

"I might take a pass on the lake today, sis." Kaleb's hand on the back of Molly's waist startled her initially, then she realized they were supposed to be together. Or at least making people believe they were together. "I think I'm going to hang out with Molly this afternoon."

"That's sweet," Kylie said, zeroing in on her brother. Uh-oh, someone wasn't fooled. "What do you guys plan to do?"

"Oh, you know. Maybe just relax." Kaleb's fingers were drawing soothing circles along Molly's lower back. "Take things easy."

The gears in her brain finally clicked into place and Molly realized what Kaleb was doing. He was playing nurse again. And it was rather insulting. But before Molly could announce to him and everyone else in the restaurant that she didn't need looking after, Kylie pointed her finger at him.

"I know what you're up to, Kaleb," she said, and Molly's stomach sank under the deep breath she'd just sucked in. "You're trying to avoid your family so you can hide out at Molly's and get a bunch of work done."

Oh, was that all? Molly slowly let out the air she'd been holding in. That wasn't exactly a secret, but she'd probably set him up for that accusation when she'd told his sister he'd been taking work calls in the bathroom. However, he deserved it after following her into the ladies' room thinking she needed to be rescued. She remembered the video chat that morning at her apartment after he'd fixed her breakfast and how that'd turned into a slew of emails and conference calls. Sure, Kaleb was legitimately overbearing in his self-appointed nursing role. She'd almost leaped up from the booth and lunged after that half-eaten cinnamon roll he'd confiscated from her earlier. But she also knew that taking care of her gave him the opportunity to take care of his own agenda.

When she was a kid, her parents used to make her oldest brother, Tommy, babysit them. He'd use money from his job at the car wash to buy a couple of frozen pizzas for dinner and a huge tub of licorice. Then he'd let all of them watch his prized VHS copy of *Top Gun* so that he could go out on the back porch with his girlfriend without his younger siblings bugging him.

"No, I'm not," Kaleb snorted, pulling her up against his side. "Molly would rather keep things low-key today. That's all."

Oh, no, that was *not* all. Kaleb was now using her as a pawn in his family avoidance game and she wasn't about to become a part of it. Especially if it meant sitting around the apartment listening to him make phone calls while she was bored out of her mind.

"Actually—" she placed a hand on his bicep and smiled sweetly at Kylie "—I would much rather go Jet Skiing with you guys."

Kaleb watched Molly peel off her cotton sundress and squeeze the top half of her bikini-clad body into a life vest. After their kiss in the ladies' room an hour ago, he hadn't trusted himself to ride in the same car with her to the lake. Instead, he stayed behind to finish his biscuits and gravy and listen to Freckles making jokes about his breakfast not being the only thing that was cooling down.

And now that he was here signing for the Jet Ski rentals, he certainly didn't intend to ride on the same watercraft with Molly. Unfortunately, since Kylie had dropped her off, it was either ride with her or ride with Bobby Junior and his six-year-old son, Bobby Three. So Kaleb sat on the Sea-Doo listening to the dock manager explain how to use the throttle while a group of college-age boys gassing up a pontoon boat ogled Molly's tan legs.

She reached up to secure her ponytail, flashing him a glimpse of her taut belly button, and Kaleb missed whatever it was the manager said about the lack of brakes. Gripping the handlebars too tightly, he accidentally revved the engine when she put her hands on his shoulders to climb on behind him.

"You ready?" he asked. She gave him a thumbs-up and they were shoved away from the dock. He tried not to notice her knees straddling his hips as he motored along slowly, following his older brother to the white buoys marking the end of the no-wake zone. This was supposed to be a family day, but after the way he'd kissed her up against the bathroom wall this morning, all he could think about was the different possible ways for her legs to end up wrapped around him.

When they hit the open part of the lake, Kaleb's thumb gunned the throttle and the sudden launch forward made Molly grab onto his waist. She shrieked and laughed and begged him to go faster. He tried to oblige, keeping a safe distance away from other boats and skiers, but after only a few minutes, she called out over his shoulder asking him to stop.

"What's wrong?" he asked after shutting down the engine.

"Nothing," she replied as she stood up, rocking the watercraft. "I want a turn to drive."

"Are you sure you're okay?"

"Kaleb, I fly million-dollar planes at mach speeds up in the air. I think I can steer a little Jet Ski at sixty miles per hour."

"I wasn't doubting that you *could* do it. Only whether you *should* do it. Did you check your blood sugar back at the dock?"

"No, but I did when I went home to change. I don't have to check it every five minutes, Dr. Chatterson." She reached over his head and grabbed onto the steering bars.

"What are you doing?" he asked from his forced crouching position.

"Switching spots with you."

"Shouldn't we pull over first?" he asked, looking at the shoreline.

"Kaleb, we're in the middle of a lake. This is as pulled over as we're going to get. Hold us steady." They rocked to the left briefly before she swung her right leg around in front of him. She brought it down on the other side and stood there straddling the seat, her rear end only a few inches from his face. "You're going to need to scoot back so I have room to sit down."

"I don't want you to sit down. I'm kind of enjoying the view from here."

She made a squeaking sound before wedging her butt against the front of his board shorts and wiggling herself backward.

"Are you trying to kill me?" he asked, finally

relinquishing control of the handlebars so that he could grab onto her hips and hold her still.

"Did you guys break down?" Bobby Junior called out as he lapped back toward them. The last thing Kaleb needed was for his brother to see him in this aroused state and then go back and tell the others. He'd never hear the end of it.

"No, we're good now," Molly yelled back before the engine roared to life. Kaleb barely had time to grab onto the seat strap in front of her before the Jet Ski lurched out of the water.

Water spray was hitting his prescription sunglasses and her hair was whipping against his face by the time she reached the top speed. God, he hoped this was the top speed because if she went any faster he'd fly off the back. She dove behind boats and jumped their wakes, spun in doughnuts and leaned into fast turns. Normally, he'd be recording notes so that he could recreate this experience in some sort of immersive video game. But for once in his life, he didn't want to miss out on the actual experience.

Kaleb decided that no virtual-reality screen or headset could mimic this very real fear of imminent death. Nor could it replicate the rush of adrenaline racing through his heart. And the slippery feel of their bodies as they slid back and forth on the wet seat, their most intimate parts colliding against each other? Forget it. Nothing would ever beat the real thing.

By the time they pulled up to the shoreline near Kylie's house, Kaleb's biceps were sore from holding on for dear life. And surprisingly, his cheeks were aching from grinning so much.

"Are you still back there?" she said, casting a saucy smile over her shoulder.

"Were you trying to make me fall off?" he asked as she turned off the engine and they coasted the rest of the way in. He took off his sunglasses and let them hang from the strap around his neck.

"Trust me. If I wanted to throw you, you wouldn't have lasted five seconds."

"Is that a fact?" he asked, gripping the plastic handle attached to the seat behind him and stretching his back. He waited for her to turn around and smile at him again, and when she did, he braced his foot on the right edge, grabbed her by the waist and tipped them over.

She was laughing when they came up from the cool water. He dove toward her and she splashed a spray of water toward his face and kicked away from him. His brothers might be world-class baseball players, but swimming was the sport he excelled at. It only took him a couple of strokes to catch her by the foot and pull her toward him.

"No fair," she said between giggles. "You're taller than me and can reach the bottom."

"So you forfeit?" he asked, drawing her closer.

"Never!"

She squirmed and wiggled against him until he had his arms locked around her. She stilled and her hands reached up to settle on either side of his face. A drop of water traveled from her temple to the corner of her lip, and as Kaleb leaned down to catch it with his own mouth, a little voice from the shore called out, "Are you gonna kiss her again, Uncle Kaleb?"

"You bet I am," Kaleb yelled back before planting a not-so-platonic kiss on her. It wasn't as long or as intense as the one they'd shared earlier today—not by a long shot—but there were children watching. And apparently everyone else in his family, he realized as one of his brothers let out a whistle.

"Hey, loverboy," Kane called out. "The Sea-Doo is floating away."

Both of them had to swim after the wayward watercraft, and by the time they pushed the thing back to shore, Molly's face was no longer as pink as her bikini bottoms. He didn't want to acknowledge that the sweetness of the latest kiss hinted at something real starting to form between them, but that didn't stop Kaleb from holding her hand as they walked up to the outdoor chairs and collapsed side by side.

Molly had never enjoyed being around another family as much as she enjoyed spending time on the lake with the Chattersons. She'd been lucky enough to be assigned to the same squadron since her graduation from the Air Force Academy, and while she had a bond with those guys, this was smaller. More intimate. Kaleb's family was fun and down to earth and didn't take themselves too seriously. And boy, could they put away the food and drinks.

She'd been careful to stay away from all the chips and snacks that Mrs. Chatterson was constantly fetching from the house. And every time Mr. Chatterson—who insisted on being called Coach—whipped up another blender full of frozen cocktails, Molly would politely refuse and grab another bottle of water.

As the sun began dipping below the mountains, Molly realized that playing on those Jet Skis all day had really tired her out. She yawned as they hauled towels and water toys to the deck upstairs. Actually, she was beyond exhausted. Her arms felt weak and her legs were sluggish.

When did she check her levels last? As the women crowded into the kitchen to give Drew tips on how to grill the carne asada for tacos, Molly excused herself to go to the restroom. She had to ask Kylie where her purse was since Kaleb's sister had brought their belongings back to the house after dropping them off at the dock earlier.

By the time she got the bathroom door closed, her forehead was damp with sweat. She sat on the closed lid of the toilet, her hands slightly shaky as she pricked her finger. Molly knew the number was going to be low before the digital screen came to life. Sixty-eight. She twisted the cap off one of the glucose gel tubes her doctor told her to carry in her black case. The heavily sweetened lemon flavor made her lips pucker as she sucked it down quickly.

Looking at the tube, Molly decided that the advertised "pleasant taste" was a load of bull. Fortunately, the rapid absorption promise was legitimate because she was already feeling better. She used the facilities, then washed her hands, holding her mouth under the faucet afterward so she could greedily gulp down more water.

When she stood up, her hands were braced on either side of the sink, her complexion slowly returning to normal in the mirror's reflection. She thought she'd been so good by not eating any junk food today. Apparently, by avoiding everything, she'd gone too far in the opposite direction.

"Ugh," she groaned at herself, stopping just short of banging her fist on the marble countertop. There was no winning with this stupid disease. The military had trained her to adapt and overcome any snafu. She was smart, she was capable of anything her instructors and commanding officers had thrown at her and she'd always been healthy and physically active, taking decent care of her body. She'd thought she'd done everything right. So why couldn't she get this damn thing under control?

Maybe because she hadn't felt like her old self since she'd gotten the diagnosis. And if she wasn't herself, then who was she? Molly inspected the person in the mirror. The one with tired eyes and sunken cheeks and fingertips that looked like pincushions. More important, if she didn't get control over things soon, what would she become?

A knock sounded at the door. Molly drew in a ragged breath and squared her shoulders before turning the knob, bracing herself to confront Kaleb on the other side. Instead, she saw Julia, Kane's fiancée.

"Is everything okay in here?" the woman, who also happened to be a Navy surgeon, asked. Molly prayed for serenity, but decided she was too cursed to be spared another interrogation.

"Never better." Molly pushed her exhausted cheek muscles into a grimacing smile. But then she followed the doctor's eyes to where the little black case lay open on the counter, the glucose meter and insulin pen all but jumping up and waving hello.

She might not officially be a Chatterson yet, but clearly Julia had been hanging around them long enough to disregard the idea of personal boundaries because she pushed past Molly and asked, "Why don't you wear a medical alert bracelet?"

Molly sighed and shut the door, hoping nobody outside the hallway powder room could hear them. "I was just diagnosed and I'm not big on jewelry so I haven't found one that I'm ready to commit to yet."

"Does Kaleb know?" Julia asked, and Molly nodded. "It certainly explains why he's always stealing your drinks or offering you Diet Cokes. Does your commanding officer know?"

"Unfortunately." A look passed between the women and Molly didn't have to explain to the military doctor that type 1 diabetes was a whole different breed from its more manageable type 2 relative, and that her need for insulin was an instant disqualification for keeping a pilot's license. "I'm supposed to be seeing a few doctors over at Shadowview and get their reports before I can appeal a medical discharge."

"How're you holding up?" The question seemed simple enough, but Molly felt her tough resolve slipping. Nobody had ever asked her that. The doctors pushed information and statistics and instructions at her. Her commanding officer asked her to keep him in the loop. She hadn't told her squadron yet because she didn't need their pity, nor did she want to be a reminder to them that even the best pilots could have their careers cut short like this. Kaleb, who was the only noncivilian that knew, seemed more concerned with trying to fix her than trying to understand her.

"I was just trying to figure that out." Molly sniffed, blinking back the tears.

"From what I understand, it can be a very lonely and confusing road." Julia put a gentle hand on Molly's shoulder.

The light touch stirred up something inside her. All

the emotions and the burdens and the worries twisted into a tornado inside her chest, swirling around and lifting into a funnel of words spilling out of her mouth.

"Every day for the past month, I'm constantly doubting myself, questioning myself, pricking myself to check to see that I haven't eaten too much or not enough. It's like taking a test I haven't studied for and no matter what the stupid number is on the screen, it's still a failing grade because it's a constant reminder that I'm going to have to live like this for the rest of my life. From here on out, I will always be a prisoner to this disease and I hate it. I resent the power these numbers have over me. It's so much easier to just avoid testing altogether and tell myself that I'm still the same person, that my body hasn't betrayed me. So I guess I'm not holding up very well at all. I've lost a piece of myself, and no matter what I do, I'll never get it back. I can never go back to what I was."

Unlike the rest of the medical professionals she'd talked to—which hadn't been all that many—Julia just nodded, a calm understanding in her eyes. And then she did the most surprising thing of all and drew Molly into a tight hug. A sob spilled out of her throat, and the next thing she knew she was crying in a stranger's arms. Yet, it felt so good to be able to just talk and have someone listen without giving advice or speaking in platitudes or trying to make things better.

When every last tear had been wrung from her, Molly stepped back and looked at her splotchy red face in the mirror. "I hate being weak."

Julia grabbed a washcloth from the cabinet below and ran it under the cool stream of the faucet. She wrung it out before handing it to Molly. "You are not weak. You might have weak moments, or even weak days. But if you keep trying and fighting, you will always come back stronger. In fact, you're about to find out exactly how strong you can be."

Another knock sounded at the door and Molly looked around the tiny half bathroom. "I don't think we can fit anyone else in here."

Julia smiled and cracked the door open. Molly heard Kaleb's hushed voice on the other side, and instead of being annoyed that he was checking up on her again, she melted. When Julia told him to wait in the hall and turned back to ask her how she wanted to proceed, Molly leaned a hip against the counter in relief. Finally, someone was letting her be in control.

"I should probably go home. But I don't want to cause…"

Another knock, but this time, Kaleb didn't wait for a reply before opening the door and letting himself in. So much for being in control.

"Did you tell her?" he asked Molly, jerking his chin in Julia's direction.

"Lower your voice, Kaleb," Julia said, trying to reach around him and squeeze the door shut. "Sorry, all the Chattersons can be a little loud and overbearing. But they mean well."

"Are you seriously comparing me to the rest of them, Julia?" Kaleb squished past his soon-to-be sister-in-law to stand closer to Molly. He put the back of his hand against her still-splotchy cheek, as if the only thing wrong with her was a slight fever. "You hardly ate anything this afternoon and your blood sugar got too low, didn't it? I had a feeling that was going to happen."

Because he was now standing between them, Molly

had to make eye contact with Julia in the mirror. "Do all of them also have a tendency to act like they know what's best for everyone else?"

"For everyone but themselves sometimes," Julia said, then gave Kaleb a slight shove when he opened his mouth to respond. "Molly was just about to tell me how *she* wanted to proceed."

"I was saying that I should ho home, but I don't want to cause a big scene." Molly twisted her lower lip between her teeth before continuing. "I, uh, haven't told Maxine or anyone else in my family yet, so…"

"Don't worry." Julia winked. "Unlike the rest of the Chattersons, I know how to keep my mouth closed. And if anyone suspects anything and asks, I can claim physician/patient confidentiality."

Except Julia hadn't acted like a doctor. She'd acted like a friend. And if she thought it odd that Molly would emotionally unload upon a complete stranger in a bath-room about things she didn't feel comfortable sharing with her own sister, the kind woman didn't mention it.

"*I* can keep my mouth closed," Kaleb muttered under his breath.

"Do you feel up to driving?" Julia asked her.

"I'll drive her home," Kaleb said, causing Julia to roll her eyes.

"Molly, what do *you* want?" she asked.

Nobody was more surprised than her when she said, "I'd prefer Kaleb take me."

## Chapter Eight

For the second time that week, Kaleb found himself shoved behind the steering wheel of Molly's cramped rental car, driving her to the apartment in downtown Sugar Falls. Julia, thankfully, had promised to come up with an excuse for their sudden departure while they slipped out the French doors of Kylie and Drew's master bedroom.

He had a million questions to ask, but he kept silent, letting Bruno Mars's soulful melody on the hip-hop station do the talking for both of them. The streetlights came on as they turned off Snowflake Boulevard, and when he pulled into the parking spot behind the bakery, Kaleb finally asked, "Are you hungry?"

"A little," Molly admitted.

"I'll come up and make you some dinner." He tried to make it sound more like an offer, but the truth was that there was no possible way he was going to leave her alone. Julia hadn't told him what they'd talked about, and while Kane's fiancée assured him that Molly was fine—physically—she'd also suggested that it wouldn't be a bad idea for Kaleb to stay the night with her. Okay, so maybe Julia hadn't come right out and made that suggestion, but he would've if he were the doctor in this situation. It was definitely implied that Molly shouldn't be alone until her levels were stabilized.

"I really miss the days of just ordering a pizza. I'm going to need to make that appointment with the dietitian because my diet is starting to get pretty limited," she said halfheartedly, not quite convincing Kaleb that she was back to her feisty self.

He was just happy that she wasn't sending him on his way. When they got inside the apartment, she yawned, then said, "Make yourself at home. I'm going to go rinse off."

Kaleb was left in the kitchen, debating whether he had enough time to download another cooking lesson on his smartphone before she got out of the shower. Then he decided that he probably shouldn't be thinking of her in the shower. He rummaged around in the fridge and found some sliced turkey and a block of Havarti… but no bread. He sliced it all up, then cut up an apple and grabbed a handful of grapes, putting it all on one platter. He inspected his culinary masterpiece. Nobody was going to offer him a contract for his own show on a cooking channel, but it'd do.

When Molly came back to the kitchen, she was wearing a short white robe, her tan legs still damp from the hot steam. "That was fast," Kaleb said.

She helped herself to some turkey and grapes as she propped her elbows on the counter. "I was too tired to wash my hair." She ate slowly while he stared at the sun-dried curls piled on top of her head in a messy ponytail.

Kaleb's lips turned down in worry. She really did look exhausted. He stacked a piece of cheese onto a slice of apple and popped it into his mouth. They were both hungry and ate in silence for a few minutes.

He found a couple of bottles of unsweetened tea in the fridge and handed one to her. "Just for the record, I like your hair like that."

"If you think this looks good, just wait until morning." Molly extended her hands a few inches away from her head. "When I wake up, it'll be out to here."

Kaleb swallowed down his last bite. If he wasn't so tired himself, he would've asked if she was suggesting he spend the night. But neither one of them were in the mood for teasing and he didn't want to give her the opportunity to argue. Instead, he simply said, "I can't wait to see it."

"Pfshh." Molly ate more turkey and he was relieved to see that over half the plate was now gone. "That's easy for you to say. Even after a day in the lake, Kaleb Chatterson, you still look perfect. Not a single, smooth brown strand out of place."

He held himself perfectly motionless as she reached out and ran her fingers over his head. But if Molly kept touching him like this, he wouldn't be able to stay still.

"Come on," he said, grabbing her hand.

"Where are we going?" she asked, although it had to be pretty obvious that he was leading her to the master bath.

"I'll wash your hair for you," he said, his voice much gruffer than he'd intended.

"How?" Her eyes suddenly seemed less tired in the

bright light of the white tiled bathroom. In fact, they almost looked determined.

"I'm sure I can think of a way." He studied the sink, then the bathtub, weighing the options. "Wait here. I'm going to go grab a cup from the kitchen."

When he returned, Molly was standing in the same spot where he'd left her. Either she was too weak to protest, or she really wanted clean hair. Grabbing a stack of folded towels, he dropped them on the tile floor by the claw-foot tub.

"Sit on these and lean back against the bath," he instructed.

Molly eyed him doubtfully, then plopped down, her tan, bare legs extending out of the center opening of white robe. Desire raced through him.

Kaleb turned on the faucet, letting the water heat up as he looked around the bathroom for some shampoo. Coming back to the tub with the bottle he found inside the glass-enclosed shower stall, he slowly sank to his knees as Molly's gaze never left him.

It took a lot of trust for someone like her, someone who liked being independent and in control, to allow another person to perform such a personal task for them. Kaleb needed to prove that he was worthy of the responsibility.

Pulling a hand towel off the nearby rack, he draped the terrycloth over the curved edged of the tub, then lifted the tendrils of hair off her neck as he guided her head back.

When he paused for a second to study the elastic band holding up her ponytail, Molly said, "Let me get it."

Her voice was low, sounding as if it came from the deepest part of her throat, and Kaleb's heart stopped as she reached up, causing the V-neck opening of the robe to gape open and revealing the silhouette of the top of one breast.

When her hair cascaded around her face, his pulse shot back to life, beating at a more frantic pace. Molly closed her eyes as he used the plastic cup to slowly poor warm water over her scalp, smoothing back strands with the palm of his hand.

Molly moaned, her relaxed shoulder pressing into Kaleb's chest as he leaned over her. Even though his fingers were trembling, he carefully massaged the shampoo against her scalp, trying to focus on evenly distributing the suds instead of watching her chest rise and fall with the long, drawn out breaths she was taking.

Kaleb didn't know how much more of this intimacy he could experience without taking things to the next level. He began rinsing out the soap, but it was a longer process to get all the lathered suds out of her curls. When he finally shut off the spout and grabbed another towel to wrap around her wet hair, Molly opened her eyes, her lids heavy, her pupils dilated.

Her voice was still throaty as she said, "Suddenly, I'm not so tired anymore."

Kaleb stood up, then held out his hand to help her rise to her feet. The towel tumbled off her head just as she looked at their reflections in the mirror. Molly ran a hand over the tangled, wet curls.

Molly turned to him and Kaleb held his breath.

Before he could say a word, she unknotted her robe and let it fall to the floor.

His heart slammed against his chest and his lungs weren't capable of expelling all the oxygen trapped inside. She'd been in a bikini all day and his brain had pushed itself to its limits imagining what was underneath. Yet, even his imagination and the tiny peeks he'd stolen earlier when her robe had loosened couldn't do her body justice. She was perfect. Her small breasts were high and proud with tight pink nipples centered like regal crowns. Her waist was tiny, which made the curve of her hips that much more round. Her legs were lean, but strong and toned. And if he looked at the spot where they joined, he would be a goner. "You're beautiful."

She blushed at his compliment before turning around and reaching inside the shower to turn on the spray. When the water heated up, she stepped in and left the glass door wide open before looking back at him and saying, "I don't know if there are any shirts here that might fit you, so unless you want to get yours all wet…"

She didn't finish her sentence, nor she didn't have to. He heard a seam rip as he yanked the cotton T-shirt over his head. And then, because it seemed like the only fair thing to do, he untied his board shorts and let them fall to the floor. He set his glasses on the edge of the sink, giving silent thanks that he wasn't farsighted, before stepping into the steamy shower with her.

Her eyes were closed as the hot water sprayed against her scalp, steam misting over their bare skin. Kaleb wrapped an arm around her waist, pulling her away from underneath the shower nozzle, then picked up the bottle of conditioner and squirted some in his palm. She put her hands on his chest, making slow wet circles against his pecs.

He massaged the cream into her hair, and as his fingers slowly worked through the tangles, she dipped her head back and moaned. He didn't trust his voice enough to say anything but her name. "Molly."

"Hmm?" she asked.

"I need to rinse you off."

Their bodies slid against each other as they changed places once again and the water sluiced through her hair, causing silky rivers to trail over her nipples and past her flat stomach. He had to bite back a groan before he managed to say, "Okay, it's rinsed."

She opened her eyes and he recognized the playful, yet determined look from when she'd wanted to drive the Jet Ski. "Now it's my turn."

She reached for the bottle of bath gel. His chest rose and fell as she took her time sliding her soapy hands across the planes of his body. Except unlike her, he watched as she washed him, not wanting to miss a second of this erotic experience. When she lifted her hands to his shoulders, she looked in his eyes and smiled. "You're beautiful, too, Kaleb."

This time, he didn't hold back the groan before bringing his mouth down to claim hers. His rigid length pressed against her stomach and their lips and hands slipped against each other as they both tried to gain traction. "Molly, you better tell me to stop or I'm going to take you right here in this shower."

"Hold that thought," she said before opening up the glass door. She stepped out without grabbing a towel and walked over to the sink. He stared at her dripping wet body as she bent to retrieve something from the cabinet underneath. When he saw the box in her hand, he didn't even bother to turn off the water before stepping out and striding across the tile floor to her. She barely had the foil packet opened when he lifted her up and set her on the counter. He stepped between her knees, and, as she rolled the condom on him, he prayed he didn't lose himself right then.

She raised her lips to his and he entered her at the same time. She gasped and he held himself still, letting them both acclimate to the feel of each other. But when she gasped and rocked her hips forward, he took the invitation. He hooked his forearms under her knees, each stroke bringing him deeper and closer to her.

He could tell by the little panting sounds coming from her throat that she was on the edge and he pulled his face back, just enough to watch her as he delivered one more fulfilling thrust.

Molly was curled up against Kaleb's side on the queen-size bed, the sheets still damp because, apparently, they didn't like wasting time with towels. He'd carried her here after their rushed coupling on the bathroom counter. He hadn't said anything about what had just happened between them and, while Molly had never slept with a man she wasn't in a relationship with, she also wasn't the kind of woman who mistook physical attraction for love.

And what had happened between her and Kaleb was pure physical attraction. Okay, so maybe the hair washing thing had been a bit intense, but only because of their mutual desire. It had been building all week and things had come to a head when they'd kissed this morning in the café. Sure, some of her raw emotions might've affected her better judgment and caused things to happen sooner than she was used to, but she'd been dealing with so many setbacks in her life lately, she needed to prove to herself that she was still a woman, capable of feeling something other than disappointment and doubt. She could still experience pleasure.

When she'd dropped her robe in front of Kaleb, she felt a rush of power and confidence that she hadn't experienced in so long. All thoughts of physical inadequacy and failure floated away and she was back in control of her body.

"Thank you," she said to him, doubting that he would ever comprehend how grateful she was in that very moment.

The muscles of his abdomen flexed as he gave off a short chuckle. "I think I should be the one thanking *you*. I've never felt so clean and yet so dirty at the same time."

She lifted her head to face him. "Just so you know, I don't always invite the men I'm platonically dating into the shower with me."

"I don't think there was anything platonic about what we just did." He smiled and she traced a finger along his bare chest. Maybe not. But that didn't mean that Molly could afford to go falling for someone when she had no idea what her future held. Not that she was falling for anyone. This was pure sex. It had to be. She had enough to deal with; she didn't need to further complicate things by adding a relationship to the mix. He cupped her chin and lifted her face up to meet his gaze. "What's wrong?"

The guy was ridiculously good at reading her emotions. So she might as well be honest with him. "I'm enjoying spending time with you, Kaleb. Even when you deprive me anything worth eating."

The corners of his lips turned down and his jaw grew hard. "But...?"

"I know that you have your own life waiting for you when you leave here." She put her finger on his lips when he started to speak. "And I'm still trying to figure out what I'm going to do with mine."

"So you don't want to make any promises while you're going through an adjustment phase?" he said around her finger.

"Ha! It's a bit more than just an adjustment phase, Kaleb." She didn't want to touch on the making promises part of his statement. Did he *want* her to make a promise? She had no business even wondering. "My career, my health, my goals, all of that is up in the air. There's so much I don't know."

"Then why don't you start looking for those answers?" he asked.

She flopped back onto the pillow. Of course it was just that simple for him. He had an army of assistants and attorneys and experts on speed dial, ready to advise him so he could solve everyone's problems. "That's what I'm trying to do. In my own way and on my own terms."

He shifted on the bed so that he was leaning over her. He gently tugged on the sheet and then lightly drew his thumb over her exposed nipple. "For someone who likes to go so fast all the time, it sure seems to me like you're taking your sweet time."

She hooked a leg around his waist and rolled him onto his back. When she rose above him, she asked, "You want to see how slow I can go?"

He smiled and slid his hands up her legs, settling them on her hips. After that, they didn't talk about speed or anything else.

## Chapter Nine

"Nobody said anything about a baby shower," Kaleb told his sister as he balanced his phone between his shoulder and his ear so he could whisk eggs. He normally would've put the device on speaker, but Molly was still sleeping in the other room and he didn't want to wake her. "So you can count me out."

"Relax, big brother," Kylie replied. "You don't have to come to the party tomorrow, but I need Mom to help with the decorations, so either you and Dad can go to the store to pick up baby shower gifts, or you can go with Molly. I know you stayed the night at her house because the truck is still at the docks, right where you parked it yesterday."

His breath came out in a defeated whoosh, releasing any further argument. "Fine. But I'm only doing it because your friend Maxine has always been nice to me. I'm not doing it for you."

"Are you doing it for her sister, who you obviously have the hots for?" Before he could deny it, Kylie began singing, "Kaleb and Molly sitting in a tree. *K-I-S—*"

"Oh, grow up," Kaleb said before disconnecting the call.

"Who aren't you doing what for?" Molly asked as she came into the kitchen, wearing a skimpy tank top and little pajama shorts. Even dressed and after three rounds of lovemaking last night, Kaleb was still aroused by her.

"My sister just volunteered us to drive into Boise and pick up gifts for Maxine's baby shower. And I use the term *volunteer* loosely."

"Together?"

"Is that a problem?" After all the togetherness they'd shared in and out of bed last night, Kaleb didn't see how it could be. But then again, he also hadn't been the one to deliver that lets-just-enjoy-spending-time-with-each-other speech last night. It wasn't that he was in the market for anything serious or long-term, either, but it was definitely a blow to his male pride to think that there was a woman out there that wouldn't consider him a good catch.

"I guess not." She sniffed at the vegetables sautéing in the pan. "But I'll have to stop at the military hospital on the way down the mountain to do some blood work and I know how you feel about needles."

He settled his hand along the back of her neck and leaned in close. "I'm going to need the promise of some sort of reward to get my mind off all the needles and baby shower talk I'm going to have to endure today."

"Maybe if you're a good boy at the doctor's, I'll get you a lollipop," she said as she pressed a kiss along his lower lip. Before he could tell her all the other things he'd rather taste, she added, "And I won't tell the rest of your family on you when you use your work laptop in the waiting room."

"Please don't remind me about my annoying relatives when I'm trying to seduce you."

"You could better seduce me by throwing out those vegetables and adding some ham and cheese to my omelet." She gave him a playful smack on his rear before heading down the hall to get dressed.

"It's a frittata," he called out.

An hour later, Kaleb didn't know how he'd gone from being a private chef to a chauffeur, but he drew the line at folding himself into Molly's tiny car for the entire ride to Boise. After eating breakfast, they drove back to the lake to get the truck. Despite Molly's insistence that she knew where they were going, he typed the address for the military hospital into the navigation system, then synced the playlist from his smartphone with the truck's radio.

"Are you ever not playing with a gadget?" she asked, tapping her fingers on the armrest.

"They're not gadgets. They're complex computerized systems that make our lives simpler."

"Kaleb, you just spent an extra twenty minutes programming a bunch of stuff we don't need for a drive that only takes half that amount of time."

He pointed to the estimated time readout on the digital map. "It actually takes thirty minutes to get to Shadowview."

"Not if I was driving, it wouldn't," she muttered.

He thought back to her trying to set a speed record on the Jet Ski yesterday. "Well, some of us would prefer to arrive at our destinations without all the blood centrifuging down to our feet because of sustained G-force acceleration."

"While it's a top-of-the-line truck—" she patted the leather dashboard "—I doubt even I could get us up to a whole G in this."

"But with all those turns going down the mountain, that's a lot of changes in velocity, which can add to the G-force."

Molly laughed. "Now I see why Kylie calls you Brainiac."

"You're only now seeing that?" he asked. He put the vehicle in gear and tried to pretend that she wasn't blatantly studying him as they drove out of the parking lot.

"Not that I'm saying I'm smarter than any of them—except maybe Kevin—but I had a lot more time to study."

"Why's that?"

"Because they were always busy with their after-school sports and I...well... I wasn't."

"You seem pretty athletic to me," Molly suggested. He lifted a brow at her, and when her cheeks turned crimson he knew she was also thinking of how he'd carried her from the bathroom counter to the bed last night. She cleared her throat and continued. "Were you just not that into sports growing up?"

"No, I was," he admitted. "But I was diagnosed with scoliosis when I was ten and wasn't allowed to play most of them, unless they were noncontact and approved by my physical therapist. I was decent at swimming, but each time I had a surgery, it would set me back."

"That must've been tough considering most of your family members are professional athletes."

"I don't mind so much now that I'm an adult, but

back when I was a kid it bugged the hell out of me. Everyone got to be on the field while I was on the sidelines watching. I think it would've been easier if I'd been diagnosed later on, after I'd already been able to prove to people that I was just as good as my brothers. But now, none of us will ever know if I could've had a different career."

"Hmm." Molly propped her chin on her fist as she looked out the window. "If it were me, I think I'd rather not know. People say it's better to have loved and lost than to have never loved at all. But I call bull on that. It sucks to get a shot at something others can only dream about, experience a feeling that's better than you ever could've imagined, know in your heart that it's what you were made to do—and then have it ripped away from you."

"So if you could go back in time ten years ago, you never would've joined the Air Force? You wouldn't have become a pilot?"

"I just don't know." Her voice was soft. "I can't see myself as being anything but that."

"I bet you'd go back and do it all over again," he said. "You're too stubborn to do anything else."

"Well, the question is totally irrelevant unless your company is currently developing the latest software for time travel," she replied, a spark of attitude pushing the sadness out of her tone.

"How do you know we're not?" he asked as he steered the truck into the Shadowview parking lot. Just seeing that big, red cross on the sign already had his heart hammering. Telling himself that he wasn't the patient did little to help.

"You're not the only one who researches stuff, Kaleb.

I looked up Perfect Game Industries and found out that if it doesn't involve crafting alternate dimensions, or shooting aliens, zombies or pirates, you can't be bothered."

Whoa. That didn't exactly sound like a compliment. He waited for her to wink or chuckle or do something that would indicate that she was teasing him. Instead, she grabbed her tote bag and opened the passenger side door.

He followed her across the asphalt and toward the large automatic glass entrance. "By the way, do you know where we're going?"

"What? You don't already have the building blueprint downloaded on your phone?" she asked, this time with a cheeky grin.

Instead of figuring out where they needed to go, he watched her as she examined the information signs with arrows pointing out the directions. Maybe he was on edge because he hated hospitals, but something about her dismissive comment about his company wasn't sitting well with him.

"Looks like the lab is this way," she said, then tugged on his hand when he stood there planted in place. He allowed her to lead the way, keeping his fingers linked with hers as they followed a maze of hallways toward the bowels of the building.

They got to a set of double doors, and when they entered the large waiting room on the other side, the smell of antiseptic and blood made Kaleb's nostrils twitch. She signed in at the desk and when she joined him on a cold plastic bench, she whispered, "You look a little pale."

"I'm fine," he sniffed, before shifting in his seat.

"The receptionist said it's just some routine blood work and won't take long. There's a lounge area across the hall and you can wait for me over there."

"I'm fine," he said again, before curling and flexing each individual finger.

"You're making me anxious with the way you're squirming in your seat and jiggling your leg like that."

He let out a snort. He wasn't that bad. "I think it'd be more supportive if I stayed."

She patted his knee. "I wasn't asking."

"Okay." He stood up. "But text me if they move you to a different room or if you get some bad news or if anything goes wrong. Sometimes, they can't find the vein and they end up poking you over and over—"

"Kaleb," she squawked, then frantically motioned her head toward a little girl who was watching them with bulging eyes as she clung to her father's arm.

"I'll just be down the hall, then." He didn't fully exhale until he was out of the waiting room. Putting his hands in his pockets, he walked to an area that said Rehabilitation Lounge.

When he went inside, the first thing he noticed was a big-screen television set with level eight of "Rookies" playing on the screen, and a wave of pride washed through him. He wished Molly was here so he could point out that his company produced sports-related video games, as well. They were even exclusively contracted with all the major franchised teams.

A young man with a bandage wrapped around his head was dressed in Green Bay Packers pajamas and sitting on a sofa, a black wireless controller in his hand as he positioned his offensive line. His opponent was the woman wearing a robe and sitting in a wheelchair, both of her legs missing below the knees.

"Hey, man," a guy sitting behind a bank of computers said to Kaleb. "Nice shirt. I had the same one when I was in junior high."

Kaleb looked down at the silk-screened image of the Pac-Man character and the sting from Kylie's earlier comment about him dressing like a fifteen-year-old boy festered.

"Don't pay any attention to him," the woman said as she blocked a virtual field goal. "He's just mad that we got here before he did and he can't watch *The Price Is Right* in HD."

"Whatever." The man stood up from behind the computer and Kaleb saw the cast that started at the guy's wrist and went up and over his shoulder. "All there is to do around this place is sit in front of a screen. It's as if they *want* to rot our brains and make us lazy. All this supposed technology out there and none of it is helping me get back to the front lines any quicker."

He passed by Kaleb, taking one last look at the T-shirt before shaking his bald head.

"You ready to go?" Molly asked from the doorway as the guy with the cast walked out.

Kaleb had never been more ready. Unfortunately, that was the exact second that Hunter and Maxine's husband, Cooper, walked in the door.

## Chapter Ten

"What are you guys doing here?" her nephew asked.

Molly saw her brother-in-law's eyes zero in on the stretchy blue bandage wrapped around her elbow and she knew the former-MP-turned-police-chief was dying to hear her answer. Her brain spun trying to come up with a plausible explanation. Was it flu shot season? Best to stick to something vague. "Just some routine stuff."

"Captain Markham!" A corpsman chose that precise moment to come into the room holding out a sheet of paper. "You forgot the printout we downloaded off your glucose meter. We already sent the data electronically to the endocrinology department."

She pried her fingernails out of her palm to take the offered paper.

"What's a glucose meter?" Hunter asked. "Is that

one of those new virtual-reality headsets for the Play-Stations?"

"Speaking of virtual reality," Kaleb said a bit too loudly as he put his arm around the boy's shoulder. "I had an idea for a new game and you're just the person I needed to brainstorm with."

Molly was left standing there with Cooper as Kaleb lead the boy to the hallway and distracted him with talk of high-tech gadgets. Her brother-in-law studied her without making a sound, as though he had a target lock on her and was deciding how and when to launch the missile.

Instead, she launched her own counterattack. "So what are *you* guys doing at Shadowview today?"

"Drew asked me to speak at one of his PTSD support groups," Cooper responded. "Hunter was out of school today and likes to come hang out in this lounge and play video games with the patients who are recovering from their surgeries."

"How fun. I mean, for Hunter. I'm sure your group isn't, um…" She glanced at the clock above the doorway. "Well, Kaleb and I better get to the store before it closes."

"It's not even noon," Cooper said, unwilling to back down. "You want to tell me what's going on, Molly?"

"Not really." She wiped a trickle of sweat off the back of her neck. Someone needed to work on the air-conditioning in here.

"You don't have to," he said, shrugging his shoulders. "Just keep in mind that I was in the Marine Corps once and the only time I ever got an indefinite leave of absence was when I was being medically discharged."

She squeezed her eyes shut and rubbed her temples.

"Nothing's official. That's why I haven't said anything to my sister yet. But I will."

"In that case, I'm not going to ask you for details because I don't want to keep anything from my wife. A word of advice, though," he said before using his chin to gesture toward his stepson. "You should probably tell Maxine before Hunter figures out that he doesn't actually want to include a glucose meter on his Christmas wish list."

Molly exhaled. "Right. I'll definitely tell her before Christmas."

Cooper just shook his head. That was still seven months away.

Whatever Kaleb had discussed with Hunter was sufficiently exciting enough to make the kid forget about why his aunt was at the hospital in the first place. She promised him a trip to Noodie's Ice Cream Shoppe later in the week and they made their goodbyes. Kaleb waited until they were in the parking lot before he brought it up.

"So did you swear Cooper to secrecy?"

"Not really. He purposely didn't ask me anything. But he clearly knows that something is up and that whatever is going on could result in a medical discharge."

"Molly." Kaleb let out a ragged breath. "You're going to need to tell her."

She swallowed down a lump of guilt. "I know. I'm going to."

"When?"

"Maybe when I know something more definite," she said as he held open the truck door for her. When he narrowed his eyes, she added, "Fine. I'll tell her after the baby shower this weekend. I don't want to make her big day all about me."

He nodded and she climbed into the cab, settling herself deep into the expensive leather seat. As he walked around to the driver's side, she let out a sigh of relief at dodging another bullet, as well as getting one annoying errand crossed off her list of things to do.

Kaleb started the engine, and as he navigated out the lot, it was obvious to see the tension finally easing out of his body. She'd noticed how fidgety and nervous he'd been earlier and regretted making him come with her. When he pulled onto the highway, Molly apologized. "I would never have expected you to go inside if I'd known how uncomfortable you would be."

"I don't know why hospitals bother me so much. You'd think that after all my surgeries, it'd be like a second home."

"How many surgeries did you have?"

"Three."

"That sounds pretty intense." She'd noticed the scar down his back when he'd taken off his life jacket out at the lake. Molly had been curious, but hadn't asked him about it at the time because she didn't particularly enjoy discussing her own medical history. She knew Kaleb wouldn't be any different. Besides, after hearing the way the Chatterson brothers all teased each other, she'd figured it would only be a matter of time before one of them regaled them all with some story involving teenage boy shenanigans. Yet, interestingly enough, nobody mentioned it. And that family mentioned *everything*.

Then, when she'd seen it last night in the shower, there'd been steam and soap bubbles and too many other body parts that required her attention. Yet, now he'd openly brought it up, so she cleared her throat and asked, "Does your back still bother you?"

He chuckled, then said, "Only when I'm being whipped around on the back of a Sea-Doo."

Shame burned her cheeks. "Why didn't you tell me?"

"Probably because of the same reason you don't go around telling people you're diabetic. I don't want people thinking that I'm limited."

"Hmm," she murmured. No, their situations weren't exactly alike, but something about Kaleb's experience resonated with her and suddenly she didn't feel like the only person who'd ever had to give up their dreams. Maybe that's why she'd connected with him initially. Either that or the way he'd filled out his jeans. Looking at the expensive denim covering his muscular thighs, she wondered if it was a lot easier to move on from what you'd lost when your fallback career involved becoming a billionaire.

Her cell phone rang and Molly was surprised to see her mother's name on the screen.

"Are you going to answer that?" Kaleb asked as he exited the freeway.

"I should. But don't say anything in the background. I don't want her asking me any questions about who I'm with."

"Am I another one of your secrets?" Kaleb's forehead creased above the frames of his glasses.

Instead of reminding him that he hadn't been all that excited when his own family had tracked him down to Maxine's apartment the evening they'd met, Molly answered the phone. "Hi, Mom."

"I'm just calling for a status update," her mother replied. Every month or so, their parents would take turns calling all their offspring to make sure everyone was safe and accounted for—like a mama duck counting her ducklings as they crossed a bridge before using her bill to nudge them off into the water to swim on their own. These were usually short conversations. After all, they had half a dozen of them to make at a time.

"I'm in Sugar Falls visiting Maxine," Molly said. Then, before her mom could ask for more details, she added, "Well, technically, I'm about to walk into a department store in Boise to buy her a baby shower present."

"Oh, that's right. I mailed her a gift card last week and could've signed your name to it like I usually do," her mom said, making Molly feel about as responsible as a five-year-old. "What are you getting her?"

"I have no idea," Molly replied, feeling about as clueless as a five-year-old, as well. She looked at Kaleb, hoping he knew what they were supposed to be picking up. But he was stoically facing the road, staying as silent as she'd asked him to. "What does she need?"

"Probably nothing. This is her second kid. Back in my day, we had a baby shower for the firstborn and then you were on your own with all the others and had to make do with whatever hand-me-downs lasted long enough."

Considering the fact that Colonel Cynthia Markham had six children and Molly was number five, a sympathy pang shot through Molly's heart. Being so close to the caboose on the secondhand train was its own challenge and she decided to get her upcoming niece or nephew the biggest, most special gift of all.

"Anyway, have fun with your sister and give me a call when you get assigned to your next duty station," her mom said in her no-nonsense tone, then disconnected abruptly without saying goodbye. It was one of the Markham family habits that Trevor's socialite mother complained about back when they were planning rehearsal dinners and seating charts. No point in using an excess of words.

"Roger that," Molly said to nobody. She tossed the cell phone back in her purse, telling herself it was a relief that her mother hadn't asked her for more details. The weird thing was that her relief felt surprisingly similar to the seed of disappointment sitting in the bottom of her stomach.

A steady beep echoed inside the cab of the truck and Molly realized that the digital map on the dash had turned into a backup camera. Her eyes squinted in confusion and she asked, "Are you seriously using the parking assist feature?"

Kaleb didn't bother to check his rearview mirror before reversing into a spot with no other cars nearby. "Why wouldn't I? It works and the manufacturer clearly installed it for a reason."

"They install it so that people like you will pay extra for a feature that you don't need."

"People like me," he repeated, his voice soft. "Right."

He exited the truck and didn't say another word as they walked inside together. It wasn't the silence that bothered Molly as much as the fact that she wasn't accustomed to Kaleb being off his smart devices and still not bombarding her with a million questions. Something wasn't right. While this shopping trip didn't fall under a routine mission for her, it wouldn't serve any purpose to have her wingman pissed off at her. "Did I insult you or something back there?"

"Nope." Instead of looking at her, he pulled out his cell phone and tapped on an app that gave the layout of the store. "The baby section is toward the back."

"Do you know what we're supposed to get her?"

"Kylie sent me a list of things to buy. But I think we're supposed to pick out our own gifts."

Right. As Maxine's sister, of course she should pick out something special. Her mother's words about signing her name to a gift card ricocheted in her head. Surely, she could decide on something as simple as a baby shower gift. It was a baby. All it could do was eat, sleep and poop.

Yet when they walked into the baby department, the sheer volume of choices overwhelmed her. How was she supposed to narrow all of this down to just one item? They passed something called a BOB jogging stroller and Molly paused. Maxine was an avid runner, so maybe something like this would work. Then she spotted the price tag and had to do a double take to make sure the thing didn't come with a four-cylinder engine and a kidney off the black market.

"Maybe we should focus on the stuff on the list first," Molly suggested.

"Right." Kaleb blew out a long puff of air. "What in the hell is a onesie?"

"Beats me. With all the kids in your family, I thought you'd be an expert at this stuff."

"Your family is bigger than mine and you don't seem to know either," he pointed out.

"Touché."

"Well, they come in a pack," he said, staring blankly at the electronic notepad on his phone. He tapped his watch and spoke into it like some secret agent. "Angela, send me a picture of a package of onesies."

"Did you seriously just tell your assistant to figure out what one of the things was on your list?"

He studied her for a moment before speaking at his wrist again. "Also, send me a picture of a diaper genie, a boppy pillow, a swaddle sack—"

Molly reached out and wrapped her hand around the face of his watch. "Why don't we just find someone who works here and ask them?"

"Because I trust Angela."

"Doesn't she have more important things to do than research baby gear?"

"Don't we all?" He dropped a light kiss on Molly's mouth and she was reminded of how they'd spent their time last night.

He pulled her closer and her heart quickened. "Good point."

Something vibrated against the side of her waist and it took Molly a second to realize that his cell phone was still in his hand. He lifted it up to see the pictures, swiping through at least twenty of them as Molly looked on.

"How much stuff does an eight-pound human being need?" he asked, echoing her earlier thought.

She pursed her lips. "This coming from a guy who is using two electronic smart devices simultaneously?"

"The voice-to-text feature works quicker on the watch, but the images come up clearer on the phone," he defended.

"You know what else comes up clearer? Asking someone who actually works here." Molly walked toward the end of the aisle looking for anyone wearing the store uniform of a red shirt and khaki pants.

After crossing over into the toy department, Molly finally honed in on a young woman restocking the board games. "Excuse me, could you help us find some stuff in the baby section?"

"Sure." The lady stood up and clipped a walkie-talkie onto her back pocket. "What are you looking for?"

"Something called a bopsie and, um, hold on. We have a list over here." She waved the clerk toward where she'd left Kaleb, who stood rooted in the center of the aisle, his eyes bouncing from his cell phone to the display racks, then back to his cell phone. Molly called out, "I brought reinforcements."

Kaleb quickly relinquished his phone over to the store employee, which was saying something since the only time she'd seen him without his phone was in the shower last night. Heat stole up Molly cheeks and she pretended to be very interested in a natural flow baby bottle that supposedly reduced colic.

"It's for a gift," he clarified.

The woman eyed Molly's flat stomach before saying, "I'm guessing you two don't have kids of your own yet?"

"Not together," Kaleb said swiftly. His eyes widened as he quickly amended, "Or separately."

Molly found herself wondering if she should've been offended by his initial instinct to clarify that they weren't a couple—or at least a couple who might produce offspring. Kaleb's tone suggested that their having babies together was ludicrous. Perhaps it was.

Instead of allowing herself to dwell on it, Molly followed Kaleb and the store clerk as the woman pointed out where all the items on their list were located. Unfortunately, that only solved the first part of the shopping conundrum because now they needed to narrow things down by colors and patterns.

After the employee left, Kaleb turned to Molly and asked, "Do you know if the baby is a boy or a girl?"

Molly racked her brain for the answer. How could she not know the sex of her expected niece or nephew? As much as it'd stung to hear the kid say it out loud, Hunter had been correct when he'd announced that the Markhams weren't the type of family who got bogged down in each other's personal business. But surely, something as momentous as a new baby would've been discussed. At her blank expression, Kaleb said, "I'll text Kylie and ask."

"Wait!" A light bulb went off in Molly's brain. "I just remembered. They're waiting to find out the gender."

She exhaled hard enough to blow a curl out of her face, relieved she was only forgetful, not completely oblivious to what was going on in her sister's life. Granted, Hunter had been the one to clue her in on that little detail when he'd stayed with her last weekend, but still. She eventually would've asked.

Needing to prove that she really did care about her family, Molly decidedly chose a pack of onesies with a neutral pattern. Once they'd selected everything off Kylie's list, Kaleb leaned against the red shopping cart and asked, "So what are *you* going to get her?"

Right. She still needed to come up with a gift. Something she could sign her name to. Something…sisterly. Her analytical mind told her that nursery furniture would be the most functional. Unfortunately, it was also the most expensive. Molly kept scanning the shelves.

"What about a crib mattress?" she asked Kaleb. It was half the cost of everything else she'd seen in the nursery section, but could still be considered a big-ticket item.

He shrugged his shoulders and Molly held her breath, wishing he'd text his assistant and ask for Angela's opinion. No such luck. Ugh. She could fly multi-million-dollar jets while firing short-range missiles with deadly accuracy. Decisiveness and confidence used to come a lot easier to her. Okay, she needed to regroup. If she were having a baby, what would she want?

Her own parents, both career military officers, rarely stretched their budget for brand-new shoes, let alone bedroom furnishings. Molly recalled her first big-girl bed, which looked perfectly fine when it was covered with Maxine's faded pink butterfly quilt. But underneath it'd had a big yellow circular stain on the mattress from when her oldest brother, Tommy, had been the first owner. She gave an involuntary shudder. Yep, that decided it. Her niece or nephew was getting their very own mattress and would be the first one to pee on it.

Molly reached for one of the plastic wrapped rect-angles lined up on the metal ledge above her head, then cursed her five-foot-four-inch frame.

"Show me which one you want and I'll grab it," he said, stepping in front of her. Oh, sure. Now he was being helpful, after she'd had to do the decision making.

"Oh. Uh, that one. I guess." She pointed to the mid-priced mattress and stood back as he easily slid the thing off the shelf and set it on the floor in front of her, balancing it between his long, smooth fingers. His hands were well-shaped and all she could think about was the way they'd brought her body to life last night. And again this morning. Molly's knees gave another slight wobble and she commanded her brain not to bug out on her.

She tilted her head to the side. To her, the mattress looked a bit thin, although Molly had slept on much worse on the last aircraft carrier she'd been aboard. "Do you think this is a good enough brand?"

"How am I supposed to know?"

"You know they have a baby registry, right?"

Molly jumped at the sound of Freckles's voice behind her. The waitress from the Cowgirl Up Café was standing alongside another woman who looked very familiar, although Molly couldn't quite place her.

"Can we borrow that list?" Kaleb asked Freckles's conservative counterpart, who was wearing a pantsuit with tasteful jewelry and a hairstyle so stiff and formal not a single strand of the bob would dare to fall out of place.

The older woman passed over some printed pages and told them, "But I already called dibs on getting Maxine the jogging stroller."

Molly leaned into Kaleb's arm to read the list, but Freckles and her friend were openly staring at them and smiling in a weird, expectant way. Whether they were trying to confirm that Molly and Kaleb were actually dating or whether they were just curious about what she planned to buy her sister, Molly squirmed under their blatant scrutiny.

"Look." She pointed at the list. "Here's something in the electronics department. Let's go take a look at that."

Molly had no idea what the item was, but at least it allowed them to make a quick escape to a different part of the store. Kaleb easily tossed the mattress that she hadn't decided on onto the top of the shopping cart and made their goodbyes.

It was then that Molly realized her mistake. The baby monitor had been easy enough to find, but Kaleb had to talk to every store employee and his assistant, Angela, before settling on a newer, more expensive model that would link to a special app on the user's phone.

Then the young man who worked in the video game department recognized Kaleb and asked for a photo. It was another hour before they were finally pushing two full shopping carts into the parking lot.

This was supposed to have been a quick and easy errand. But she was finding out that nothing about Kaleb Chatterson was easy at all.

## *Chapter Eleven*

After arguing with Molly for a solid ten minutes about physics and mechanical engineering, Kaleb went back inside to buy a coil of rope so that all their purchases wouldn't fly out the back of the truck.

"I still think all of this is overkill," Molly told him when he secured the last knot.

"I like being prepared."

"You probably were an excellent Boy Scout."

"I would have been if…" He trailed off at the memory.

"If what?"

"I wasn't allowed to go to the scouting camp like my brothers. I spent a whole summer in a traction bed once reading the handbook, though, and learning how to pitch a tent, start a fire and tie ropes. I never got around to doing the first two, but I'd used up a couple of spools of dental floss practicing the more complicated knots. Anyway, I quit going to the den meetings because I didn't see the point in hanging out with a bunch of kids learning how to do things I could research and learn about at home."

"I'm surprised your parents just let you quit."

"I think they were initially overwhelmed with having a kid who wasn't perfect. I don't mean that they didn't love me," he rushed to say when he saw her horrified expression. "In fact, they probably loved me too much because they treated me with kid gloves. Even my brothers took a hiatus from picking on me. But don't worry, they bounced back after my first surgery when the doctor told them that I actually needed to exercise in order to get better. Of course, I still wasn't allowed to do the contact sports, but my dad found a swim coach and I had daily strengthening workouts. By the end of middle school, I could easily outdistance any of my hot-shot baseball-playing brothers in the pool."

She smiled at him before getting into the passenger seat. "Being a kid sister, I'm pretty impressed that you were able to beat them at something."

He walked around to his side of the truck and climbed in. "Ha. Apparently, you've never raced against a Chatterson. They're horrible at losing. Kane and Kevin started going to practice with me during their off-season so they could challenge me to a rematch."

"Yeah, I caught a glimpse of your family's competitiveness when they were playing badminton at the barbecue on Wednesday." Molly smiled as he started the engine. "Yesterday, Kylie was still sporting that bruise from that shuttlecock Bobby Junior served during the last match."

"Trust me, they've really mellowed out since we were teenagers."

"So did they ever beat you at swimming?"

"Kevin did once, but only because he reached over into my lane and grabbed hold of the waistband of my Speedo."

"That's horrible," Molly said, but the words were muffled by her giggles.

"You have no idea. The girls' water polo team was meeting for tryouts and were all on deck and watching."

Molly's nose was practically touching her knees, she was bent over laughing so hard. When she'd wiped the tears from her upturned cheeks, she asked, "Did he get in trouble?"

"Yeah, he got grounded for two weeks. One week for cheating and one week for embarrassing me. Although, he had an out-of-state baseball tournament during the second half of his punishment and I decided that justice wasn't exactly being fulfilled."

"You mean you took matters into your own hands?"

Kaleb shrugged his shoulders. "I might've hacked into his computer account and printed out some of his correspondence to a certain high school junior who he had this huge crush on."

"Were the emails pretty scandalous?"

"Unfortunately, no. They'd mostly been sharing pictures of cute kittens and discussing civics homework. But it taught him that I would always be one step ahead of him when it came to technology. Anyway, I'm starving. How're your levels? Should we go grab a bite to eat?"

Kaleb silently cursed himself when the smile suddenly left her face. He hated that he'd gone and ruined their playful banter with that reminder, but someone had to look out for her health. Molly hadn't had a meal since she'd only managed to swallow down a few bites of the well-done frittata he'd made. Not that he could blame her. The online video didn't say anything about baking times being converted for the high altitude.

Without replying, she pulled the black case out of her purse and pricked herself. He put the truck in gear to avoid staring at her, knowing how it felt to be the subject of strict medical scrutiny. Yet he couldn't stop himself from holding his breath until she told him the number.

"Kane told me about a restaurant near this shopping center. It's called the Bacon Palace. Does that sound good?"

"It does, but—" she looked out the back window "—I don't think we should leave all this stuff in the bed of the truck. Someone could steal it."

"Right." Personally, Kaleb didn't see what anyone would want with a bunch of random baby gear, but he'd hate to have to go back to the store and find all those items again. He pulled into another parking spot and tapped on his cell phone screen.

"What are you doing now?"

"I'm searching for nearby drive-through restaurants."

"Or you could just lift your head and look at the big signs on the side of the road. We passed at least several of them on the way here."

"Yeah, but I have this app that shows the menu and the guest ratings so we don't waste our time going to somewhere that isn't good."

"Kaleb, it's fast food. I think you're going to need to lower your billionaire expectations for at least one meal."

Billionaire expectations? What was that supposed to mean? First, his sister made fun of his cheap shirts and now Molly was making fun of his financial situation. Someone needed to pick a lane. "Do I come across as some sort of snob to you?"

"Not a snob exactly. But sometimes you can get a little controlling about how you want things done. Don't you ever just live in the moment? Do something without a plan or a map or a phone call to your assistant?"

"Fine," he said, rolling his stiff shoulders backward in an effort to loosen them. "Let's just fly by the seats of our pants and go to the first place we see."

"This is killing you, isn't it?" Molly smiled at him as he pulled out of the parking lot. The dare in her eyes was the only thing that kept his fingers away from the navigation screen.

"Nope. I'm great. Call out a restaurant as soon as you see it."

"There's a place called Burger X-Press," she suggested.

"I don't trust businesses that can't spell out their full name."

"Across the street is Big Smokey's Pit House."

"It looks closed," he said, ignoring the fact that the lights were on, a cloud of barbecue smoke was billowing from the roof and the parking lot was packed.

"Krispy Kreme." She pointed to the giant doughnut-shaped entrance sign. "That counts as a drive-through."

"You wish," he said.

She nodded at a take-out building shaped to look like a giant taco. "How about Señor Shaddy's Taco Shack?"

"That shack looks like one of those places where people used to drop off their pictures to get developed."

They continued another block before she asked, "Fantastic Falafels? Or do you have something against alliteration?"

"I'm good with that." He made a casual shrug and flipped on the turn signal. What he didn't say was that before she'd shamed him into closing out his phone app, this restaurant was the first one to pop up and he'd already seen its four-and-a-half-star rating.

There was also an outdoor take-out window and picnic tables with orange-striped umbrellas, so they could still keep an eye on the truck in the parking lot as they ate. He bit his tongue when she ordered the falafel platter with a regular pita, instead of the whole-wheat option. And she didn't make fun of him when he asked the virtual assistant feature on his watch how to pronounce *gyro*.

It was almost rush hour and she asked if she could drive the truck back to Sugar Falls because it had been a while since she'd been behind an engine with more than four cylinders. But the memory of Molly racing around on the Jet Ski still had Kaleb's muscles clenching, so he told her she could be in charge of the radio instead.

They were halfway up the mountain when he lowered the volume and asked if they could listen to something with a little less bass. "It makes me feel like I'm at a dance club in Vegas."

"Do you go to a lot of dance clubs?" she asked.

"Never."

"Why am I not surprised?" Molly's smile was teasing, but all day long he'd had a weird feeling that he was the butt of some sort of joke nobody was telling him about. Maybe it was all the teasing he'd been taking from his siblings recently. Or maybe it was that soldier's comment about his juvenile shirt at the rec lounge at Shadowview. Or maybe it was the fact that he'd never slept with a woman and then spent the entire day with her afterward. All he knew was that he hadn't been this insecure since high school.

He pulled into his sister's driveway and the first thing he noticed was the lack of cars parked in front, although the lights were on inside. His chest expanded and he let out a relieved breath. Hopefully, most of his family would be gone and they'd be able to drop off the baby presents and escape another evening filled with smart-aleck Chattersons.

No such luck, he realized when he swung open the front door and saw the chaos bouncing around the great room. One of Kylie's twin daughters was lying in her playpen chewing on the corner of a Dr. Seuss book, the other was sliding halfway out of her swing. Aiden and Caden Gregson were in the kitchen, stirring something in a big pot over a lit stove while a boy Kaleb had never seen before sat on the counter beside them giving them instructions. Two of Bobby Junior's kids were jumping on the huge sectional sofa, which was suspiciously missing all of its cushions.

A major-league baseball game played on the big-screen TV, the volume turned way up, but there was no other sign that another adult was present. Kaleb grabbed his cell phone, prepared to call 9-1-1.

"What's going on, guys?" Molly hollered over the noise.

"We're making chili goulash," the nine-year-old twins in the kitchen called out in unison.

"We're practicing gymnastics." One of the redheaded

girls used the arm of the couch to do a backflip onto the wooden floor.

The baby in the playpen blew a slobbery raspberry.

Molly jogged over to rescue the other baby, whose diapered rear end was now dangling out of the swing.

"Who's supposed to be in charge?" Kaleb finally asked, now that it seemed like everyone was accounted for.

"Uncle Kevin is," the extra boy sitting on the counter said. Was his family suddenly multiplying and nobody had told him?

"I'm down here." His brother waved from underneath the poorly constructed blanket fort on the living room floor. "Trying to watch the game in peace."

"Kaleb," Molly said as she looked around, holding a baby on her hip. "I think one of the kids is missing."

Kaleb did a quick headcount as Kevin climbed out from his hiding spot. "Who's missing?"

His brother pointed around the room as he called, "One, two, three, four, five, six, seven. Nope, everyone's here."

"Um, Kevin." Kaleb nodded toward the dark-haired boy. "That's not Bobby Three."

"I'm Choogie Nguyen." The kid waved a box of macaroni at him before dumping it into the pot on the stove. "I live next door."

"Okay, back to my original question." Kaleb turned toward his brother, who was now sitting on the cushionless sofa muttering something at the umpire on the TV. "Who is supposed to be in charge?"

Kevin glanced around the room, then shrugged. "I am."

That couldn't be right. Nobody would put Kevin in

charge of a load of laundry, let alone seven children. Aiden—or was it Caden?—stepped off his chair in front of the stove.

"Well, our parents went out for a date night so Aunt Kylie told them to drop us off over here. Then she and Gramma Lacey had to go to the party-supply store because Grampa Coach bought bridal shower decorations instead of baby shower decorations. One of Uncle Drew's patients called him with an emergency, so he had to leave. And Uncle Bobby is in the back bedroom talking to his wife on the phone." The kid glanced at the two girls doing cartwheels way too close to the coffee table and lowered his voice to a whisper. "Aunt Kylie said she thinks they're gonna get a *D-I-V-O-R-S-E*, but we're not allowed to say that word in front of his kids."

Molly carried the baby she was holding over to the playpen and set her down inside before taking away her twin sister's chewed book. God bless the woman for not running out the front door.

"So where's Dad and Bobby Three?" Kaleb asked his brother as he began tossing cushions back onto the sofa. It wasn't his fault that Kevin wasn't quick enough to dodge the one flung at his face.

"Oomf." Kevin hurled it back at him. "Dad took him to pick up some ice cream. You want me to call them and tell them to bring extra for you and your girlfriend?"

Kaleb felt a flush spread up his neck at his brother's purposeful use of the term. But Molly hadn't heard him or else was doing a really good job of pretending she hadn't.

"No. We're just dropping off the stuff for the baby shower." He walked over to Molly and whispered, "Do you mind if we hang out for a few minutes until a responsible adult comes back? I'm afraid someone might call child services on us if we leave them alone with Kevin."

She chuckled and it caused the warmth to spread from his neck to the rest of his body. "I don't have anywhere else I need to be."

"Is it true that you're Uncle Kaleb's girlfriend?" Caden, or possibly Aiden, tugged on Molly's hand.

Now her cheeks were the ones turning crimson. "Um…"

She looked at him with pleading eyes but before Kaleb could answer, Kevin muttered, "Not if she's smart, she's not."

"But you have to be smart to be a combat pilot, right?" Caden asked.

"Well, I did have to go to college and I like to think I'm pretty smart." Molly smiled through her confusion.

"Are you as smart as Uncle Kaleb? Aunt Kylie calls him a Brainiac," the other twin said as he walked over.

"Why does she call him a Brainiac?" Choogie, the neighbor kid, asked as he joined them in the living room.

"Because Uncle Kaleb is a computer genius and a gazillionaire and invented 'Blockcraft.'"

"I'm not allowed to play video games," Choogie announced. "Both of my moms say that junk will rot my brain."

And the ball of insecurity in Kaleb's stomach grew, making him blurt out, "Actually, there are no scientific studies that back that up."

He knew that not everybody was sold on the successful educational game he'd developed as a counterpart to the more recreational Alien Pirates series. But this was twice in the same day that someone had referred to his creations as mind-rotting junk. Of course, maybe his brain *was* rotting if he was standing here defending his life's work to a nine-year-old.

"So then if you're smart—" Caden continued his conversation with Molly "—does that mean that you're *not* Uncle Kaleb's girlfriend?"

"It's, um, complicated," Molly said before brightening up.

"Do you have another boyfriend?" Aiden asked. "Uncle Bobby told Gramma that his marriage was complicated and Aunt Kylie said that's because his wife has another boyfriend and wants a *D-I-V*—"

"No," Molly interjected quickly when she saw one of Bobby Junior's daughters somersaulting toward her. "I don't have another boyfriend."

"Have you ever had one before?" Choogie asked.

"Wow." Molly's smile was frozen as she widened her eyes at Kaleb. "Your family sure asks a lot of questions."

Technically, the neighbor kid wasn't part of his family, but Kaleb was curious about the answer himself so he just lifted his eyebrow at her. *Well?*

She let out a long breath. "I used to have a boyfriend, but we broke up."

"When?"

"Why?"

Molly gulped, but Kaleb was enjoying this too much. "Because he liked Chinese food and I didn't."

Seven sets of eyes—including Kevin's—gawked at Molly. It would've been eight, but one of the babies had fallen asleep. What did somebody's meal preferences have to do with anything?

"Do *you* like Chinese food, Uncle Kaleb?" one of the boys asked.

"Sometimes." Kaleb decided it was time to bail Molly out. "But it doesn't matter because Molly and I are just friends."

"Friends don't kiss," Aiden argued. "And we all saw you guys kiss right there in the middle of the lake. Even Coach Grampa saw it and said—"

Molly sniffed at the air. "Is something burning?"

"The chili goulash!" one of the boys hollered as he ran to the kitchen and turned off the stove.

Thankfully, Kaleb's mom and sister walked in the door at that exact moment. He tugged on Molly's hand. "Okay, so we were just dropping off the presents for the baby shower. Now that some responsible adults are here, I'm going to take Molly home."

"Don't you guys want to stay for dinner?" Lacy Chatterson asked.

"We already ate."

"Are you staying at your girrrrrrlfriennnnnnnd's house tonight?" Kevin asked, and their mom smacked him on the back of his head. "Gah, Ma! I'm missing a doubleheader today because Kaleb demanded we take our family vacation right in the middle of the season. The least I can do is give him some grief for not spending any time with us."

"All you kids ever do is give each other grief…" his mom started, and Kaleb pulled Molly toward the door.

They were just about to the truck when his sister came out onto the front porch and yelled, "We have a big day tomorrow, Molly. Make sure my brother lets you get a good night's rest!"

## Chapter Twelve

Molly was still trying to process everything as they drove back to her apartment. As they passed Duncan's Market, she finally said, "So I guess your whole family now knows that we're sleeping together."

Kaleb sighed. "Yeah, sorry for all the questions and wisecracks back there. My family isn't used to me bringing a woman around."

"You mean you've never brought a girlfriend home to meet them?"

"Can't you see why?" he asked.

"I think your family is fun."

"They're a blast. To everyone who didn't have to grow up with them or constantly have them up in their personal business."

"Well, I grew up with a family who kept to themselves

all the time. You should be glad they're nosy. It means they care about you."

"Maxine seems to care about you," Kaleb replied, bringing stirring up Molly's guilt again.

"I know she does. But it's different between us. We love each other, but your siblings are more vocal about it. More affectionate. They don't hesitate to actually *show* their love."

Kaleb snorted. "How? By annoying me?"

"That's part of what makes them so enjoyable," Molly wiggled her eyebrows. "But, seriously. Haven't your girlfriends wanted to meet them?"

"I try to go out with the women who are only interested in where I'm taking them and whether or not there will be a red carpet there."

Molly puzzled over his response for a few moments. "So you don't like women with substance? Or you purposely only date shallow women so you don't have to do serious relationships?"

"Asks the woman who broke up with a guy because he liked Chinese food."

She shifted in her seat so that she could look out the window. "What I didn't say was that our breakup had more to do with *who* I caught him eating Chinese food with. I'll give you a hint. It wasn't me."

"Ouch. How long ago was that?"

"A few days after I was first diagnosed." She used her finger to draw a zigzagging pattern along the leather of the armrest.

The car noticeably slowed down and she guessed that Kaleb had taken his foot off the gas pedal. He did that every time he felt compelled to better understand something. "You mean he cheated on you when he found out that you had diabetes?"

"No, he didn't know about my condition. Still doesn't. I showed up at his house to tell him because I figured he deserved to know that I was no longer the same woman he planned to marry. And that's when I caught him with his fortune cookie already unwrapped."

She heard the gurgle of him swallowing back his laughter and he resumed driving. But after a few seconds, she knew his silence was too good to last. "Okay, so back up. You were going to get married?"

Molly already had one strike against her with all the complications that came along with the whole diabetes diagnosis. It was humiliating to admit that she'd also been stupid enough not to know that her fiancé had been cheating on her, as well. "Do we really have to talk about this right now?"

"Let me guess, this is also something you're keeping from your sister?"

"Actually, Maxine knows about Trevor. My whole family does, since we'd already sent out the wedding invitations before I called it off. In fact, that's why my sister thinks I'm in town. To take a break and mend my broken heart."

"So this was all pretty recent?" he asked. "Does that make me the rebound guy?"

"No!" she exclaimed. "There wasn't anything to rebound from. To be honest, I'd been having reservations about going through with the marriage, anyway. I don't think I ever really loved him. Otherwise, I would've been more upset about the other woman. He was also a pilot, assigned to another squadron, so our relationship was easy and he never demanded anything from me.

My parents' marriage is the same way so I've never really known anything different. But now that I've been spending time with Maxine and Cooper and all the head over heels in love couples in *your* family—with the exception of Bobby Junior, I guess—it's become clearer that marrying Trevor would've been a huge mistake."

He pulled into the parking spot near her rental car in the alley. He didn't make a move to get out of the truck, but he'd never been the type before to wait for an invitation. Was he suddenly changing his mind about spending time with her? Her chest sunk with disappointment.

When he didn't say anything, she tried to joke, "Now if I could get the rest of my life clearer, then maybe I'd be back in business."

Finally, he reached his hand across the center console and picked up her hand, bringing it to his mouth for a soft kiss. "Just for the record, I wouldn't mind if this was a rebound thing, but I'm glad it's not."

Thankfully, he didn't ask what "this" was between them. Because Molly had no idea. All she knew was that she wasn't quite ready for it to be over.

"So are we just going to sit down here all night or are you going to come upstairs and make sure I get a good night's rest?" she asked.

He smiled before turning her wrist over and planting another tender kiss there, as well. And then nobody got any rest after that.

Molly tugged the top of her strapless sundress back into place as she looked around at the other women clustered into friendly groups, drinking prosecco sangrias and discussing their own pregnancies and labors. So far, nobody had been able to beat Cessy Walker's—Molly *knew* she'd recognized the woman with Freckles at the store yesterday—story about her water breaking at a Barry Manilow concert and her refusal to leave until after the singer's encore performance of "It's a Miracle."

Baby showers must be quite the social event in Sugar Falls because the back room of Patrelli's Italian restaurant was at full capacity and all the ladies were wearing their best pastels and floral prints. Molly had borrowed a dress from Maxine, but the ill-fitting clothes were not only a reminder of the fact that she didn't own a suitable wardrobe for a ladies' luncheon, but that her recent weight loss was most noticeable in her chest.

Kylie clinked a spoon to her glass of fruit-filled sangria. As the room quieted, Molly desperately wished she could have just one sip. More for the sugar buzz than the alcohol content. Instead, she stuck to her unsweetened iced tea.

"Okay, everyone. We're going to start our first game," Kaleb's sister announced.

Molly would've pumped her fist if it she could do so without letting her dress slip. She might not be able to drink the fancy cocktails or discuss childbirth or even contribute to the latest Sugar Falls gossip, but finally there was something she *could* participate in. She thrived on healthy competition and didn't care whether it was a combat mission or a game of gin rummy back in the barracks. She liked to win. And it had been so long since she'd won something.

Kylie passed out papers as she explained the rules of the game. "When I call time after five minutes, everyone drop your pens. The person who knows the most about Maxine wins."

Molly's face went slack as the blood rushed to her

feet. Couldn't they compete at something she'd actually be good at?

"It's not fair if you and Mia and Maxine's sister play because you guys know her the best," one of the ladies called out. Molly recognized her as the owner of the gas station and the mother of the boy who'd asked Kaleb for his signature outside the Cowgirl Up Café. The woman didn't even know Molly's name—only that she was Maxine's kid sister. But she was right, on at least part of her complaint. Kylie and Mia were Maxine's best friends and could easily win this game. Molly doubted she could even get half the answers right.

"Of course the three of us aren't playing," Mia said as she handed out pens. "We're the ones who came up with the questions."

They were? When had they done that? Molly recalled their meeting at the Cowgirl Up a few days ago. They'd briefly discussed what they intended to play, but when exactly had they… Oh. Her cheeks heated. They must've come up with the list when she'd been in the ladies' room making out with Kaleb.

As the guests began writing, Molly maneuvered herself to where Kylie and Mia were huddled. Hopefully, they had the answer sheet with them and Molly could sneak a quick peak. How sad was that? She had to rely on a cheesy baby shower game to gain a little insight into her big sister.

Better to just paste a neutral expression on her face and make herself less conspicuous. Oh, look. The gift table could use some rearranging. Molly walked over and sorted the packages in order of size, bringing the small items toward the front of the table.

"Sixty more seconds," Mia announced.

Freckles waved her sheet over her head. "I've already finished and you might as well give me the prize."

Several women groaned, because of course the waitress from the local café knew everything about everyone.

Molly held herself still while Maxine read off the answers. "Biggest craving is salt-and-vinegar potato chips."

Well, that was no surprise. Anyone with eyes and standing in the same room as her sister would've guessed that.

"Circumference of my stomach is currently forty-two inches."

Yeah, Molly would've gotten that, too, because the turboshaft in the first jet she'd flown was that exact same size.

"Does 'Tears of a Clown' count as a favorite lullaby?"

Duh. Growing up, their CD player at home always had a stack of Maxine's favorite Motown discs on it. And Hunter always sang Smokey Robinson songs as he got ready for bed.

"Foot size?" Maxine continued. "I'm still wearing my size eight shoes, but they're getting tighter."

In addition to the sundress, Molly had had to borrow a pair of wedge sandals from her sister for this party, so she would've gotten that answer, as well.

And everyone correctly wrote down that Maxine had met Cooper through her son, Hunter, because of a pen pal program at school. Hmm, maybe Molly knew more about her sister than she'd thought.

Her heart resumed its normal pace and she eased herself closer to Mia and Kylie's side, suddenly feeling less like an outsider. When lunch was served, she skipped Patrelli's famous garlic knots in the buffet line, instead loading up on the antipasto salad. Afterward, she volunteered to cut and serve the red-velvet cake so that nobody would notice that she was the only person in the room who wasn't enjoying a slice. Although she did lick some of the cream cheese frosting off her finger when she was done passing out the plates.

"So what about you?" Elaine Marconi asked Molly when she finally resumed her seat at the head of the U-shaped table by her sister. "Are you planning to have kids, too?"

The spotlight was suddenly thrust onto Molly's flaming cheeks and she turned to Maxine, looking for some sort of signal on how she should handle such a personal question. Unfortunately, her sister was distracted by something Mrs. Chatterson was saying to her.

Molly knew this was a small town, but why did people think it was appropriate to ask others about their procreation plans? Or, in her case, a lack of them. Molly took a big gulp of her iced tea. "Not any time soon."

"No, of course not *now*," Elaine replied. "You and Kaleb should take some time to get to know each other first, but maybe after your wedding."

Her eyelids popped open. What wedding? They weren't even dating. Well, they sort of were, but it was only temporary. And just for appearances. It certainly would never get to the point where they would ever need to discuss the possibility of babies.

"Not everyone wants to have kids." Julia, Kaleb's soon-to-be sister-in-law, came to her rescue. "I know Kane and I have our hands full taking care of our dog."

"That's a shame," Cessy Walker said to Julia. Molly

moved to the edge of her seat, getting ready to defend her new ally. Then the woman added, "Your and Kane's babies would be a lot cuter and smarter than that dog of yours who keeps lifting his leg on my Lexus tire every time you walk him downtown."

"Sounds like a pretty intelligent dog to me," Maxine whispered to Molly, who fought the urge to giggle because she wasn't yet convinced that this conversation didn't have the potential to take a judgmental turn. Some women had a tendency to think every other female should follow their example. It was one of the reasons Molly had loved being in a male-dominated profession. Yet, before Molly could prepare her plan of defense, someone else jumped in.

"Our son is smart and beautiful," one of Choogie Nguyen's moms said. "And he doesn't have either of our DNA."

Carmen Gregson lifted her glass of sangria. "Cheers to that. I couldn't love the twins more if they'd come from my own body."

"I never had kids," Freckles said as she helped herself to the rest of Cessy Walker's cake. "And to be honest, I don't regret my decision."

Molly had not been prepared for this. It wasn't so much that any of the women were explicitly protecting her. But they were being open and honest with their feelings and their situations and nobody was trying to pretend to be anything they weren't. Well, except for Elaine Marconi, who kept her judgmental chin firmly in the air.

"So who's ready for another game?" Mia asked, and Molly settled back into her seat as her cohost explained the rules for the blindfolded diaper races. The rest of the shower passed in a flurry of laughter and friendly competition and oohing and ahhing over presents of hand-knitted blankets and tiny, delicate outfits.

When Molly won the bingo game for having five gifts in a row on her card, she traded prizes with Freckles, who'd earlier been awarded a gift certificate to a free kayaking lesson from Russell Sports.

"Are you sure you don't mind switchin'?" the waitress asked as everyone helped clean up all the discarded bows and wrapping paper.

"I'm positive." Molly put up a hand to assure her. "I won't be in town long enough to use up a month of free yoga classes at Mia's studio."

"I wish you could stay that long," Maxine said beside her, catching Molly off guard with a one-armed hug around her waist.

"You do?" Molly searched her sister's face.

"Of course I do. I love you, Moll Doll."

The childhood nickname sent a funny flutter through her tummy and she couldn't stop herself for leaning into Maxine's side.

"Hold it right there," Kylie said before using the camera on her phone to snap a photo.

"Make sure you send me a copy of that," Maxine said to her friend before turning to Molly. "I can't remember the last time we took a picture together."

It wasn't accusatory, but since her sister had lived in the same city for the past twelve years, Molly knew that it was her own career and her countless relocations that had kept them apart for so long. Everyone smiled at their sentimental display of sisterhood bonding but the guilt weighing on Molly's shoulders made her feel like a fraud.

At least it did until her nephew and brother-in-law walked into the room and Hunter announced, "Hey, Aunt Molly, we played golf with Kaleb today and I told him about this awesome idea I had for his next video game. He's going to bring you over to our house for dinner tonight so we can talk about it."

## Chapter Thirteen

Kaleb's lower spine had barely made it through the eighteenth hole when he finally asked Hunter—who thought the sport of golf was slow and boring and only perked up when he got to race Kevin in the golf carts—to drive him back to the pro-shop for a package of ibuprofen and an Icy Hot patch while everyone stayed behind for a postgame putting match. Before Cooper and the rest of the Chatterson men met up with them for a round of beers and Reuben sandwiches, Molly's nephew had proposed a decently thought-out plan for the development of a new concept game.

The twelve-year-old invited him over to dinner at Maxine's so they could talk to Molly about the plan. Since he'd spent the past two nights at her apartment, Kaleb didn't want the woman thinking this was becoming a habit. In fact, when he'd kissed her goodbye this morning before she'd left to help set up for the baby shower, he no longer felt like they were role-playing.

When he headed back to Seattle in a couple of days, they were going to have to break up—or at least make the pretense of breaking up. He didn't know what to call it anymore. Whatever was going on between them still wasn't real, but they'd definitely crossed that platonic line and now the only awkward part of their relationship was the fact that it no longer felt awkward.

So he'd purposely not made plans to meet her directly after the baby shower, knowing that spending less time together was the key to getting their lives back to normal. But when the babysitter Kylie had hired called Drew and Bobby Junior to tell them that two, possibly three, kids appeared to have poison ivy, Kaleb sent Molly a text asking if she wanted to ride together to Maxine and Cooper's.

"So what's this big plan Hunter wants to tell me about?" Molly asked when she opened the apartment door. She was wearing snug white jeans and a light blue sweater and looked so much more comfortable than she had in the sundress she'd had on this morning when she'd left.

"It's actually not that big of deal, but he made me promise to wait until we got over there to tell you about it."

"Since when does Kaleb Chatterson wait for anything?"

"Since I saw you in those jeans," he said, sliding in close to her and putting his hands along her rib cage before giving her a kiss hello. She was wearing that mango coconut lotion again, and as his thumb brushed against the underside of her breast, she gave a soft moan. "Maybe we can be a little late."

"You know that if we're not there by six, Hunter is going to blow up both of our phones with text messages demanding to know what's taking so long. So if I have to wait to hear about this big plan, then you can wait until after we come home to finish this."

Home. He'd never trusted a woman's motives enough to let her into his inner circle, let alone live with one. Yet, the amount of time he spent with Molly felt so natural to him, so right, he didn't want to stay with anyone else. The word *home* should've scared him but instead of dwelling on it, he pushed for a more playful tone. "People are going to talk if they know you keep begging me to spend the night."

"Begging?" She grabbed her tote bag and he stepped aside as she locked the door. "I heard all about the poison ivy so don't pretend that you weren't hoping to catch another reprieve from your family over here. Besides, people are already talking."

"I'm not *only* over here for a reprieve, you know." He followed her down the stairs.

"You proved that in my bedroom last night. And the night before that," she said saucily over her shoulder. But before his ego could grow too much, she added, "It just so happens to be a bonus that since you don't have any employees here to boss around, you can also get your CEO fix by constantly micromanaging my levels and monitoring what I'm eating."

He grabbed her hand, forcing her to stop and turn around. "Do you really think I'm trying to micromanage you? Like you're some kind of project for me?"

She tilted the corners of her lips into a smirk, but it

didn't quite reach her eyes. "Well, I know it's not for my Wi-Fi since you always bring that ridiculous portable satellite thing over with you. Luckily, I don't have insecurities about the type of internet availability I can provide my guests."

Kaleb cupped her cheek. "What you lack in Wi-Fi capabilities, you more than make up for with the way your mouth does that thing—"

His watch let out a shrill ding. He yanked his hand back and silenced the ringer, but not before she had to tug on her earlobe and rotate her jaw. "Talk about overkill. Does that stupid device even serve a purpose? I mean, other than to make me go deaf?"

"Sorry," he said, then laughed when he saw the text message pop up on the screen. "But you were right about Hunter looking for us if we didn't show up on time."

He opened the passenger door for her and waited until he pulled onto Snowflake Boulevard before asking her if her hearing had returned.

"What?" she said playfully, then smiled.

"So you mentioned something earlier about people already talking about me spending the nights. What are they saying?"

"Actually, it was only one person who brought it up, but she did it in front of everyone at the baby shower and in this really uncomfortable context. But don't worry. The conversation ended up going in a different direction and I was saved from responding."

"You know that you didn't exactly answer my question, right?"

"You're doing that micromanaging thing again." She wagged a finger at him.

"And you're doing that thing where you avoid giving details so you can pretend everything is fine."

She grunted and let her head fall against the back of the seat. "She asked me if we were planning to have children."

"Together?" His stomach did a somersault and he had to command his foot to return to the accelerator. That had been his same response to the employee at the department store yesterday. Why did the idea of having children with Molly keep popping up in his mind?

"Actually, she asked if I wanted to have them, then implied that you and I had plenty of time to figure that out."

"*Do* you want kids? I mean, in general. Not necessarily with me."

She shrugged. "I don't know. I mean, I always assumed I'd have them someday, but now I don't even know if I can. Anyway, it's not something I need to figure out right this second."

"But you know you're going to have to think about your future eventually." Kaleb was only pointing that out because he wanted her to be receptive to Hunter's idea. And because he wanted her to think it was brilliant. That *he* was brilliant. He couldn't explain this sudden urge to prove that he was more than just the technology dependent overgrown kid people had accused him of being lately.

Her response was to roll her head in his direction and give him a pointed look. Not that he could blame her.

They didn't speak the rest of the way, but when they pulled into the driveway, Molly asked, "Who's car is that?"

"Maxine, don't you think it's a little weird that your former mother-in-law comes over to family dinners with your new husband?" Molly whispered to her sister in the kitchen as they heated up the leftover food from Patrelli's. Cessy Walker, the woman in question, was in the living room overseeing the men's assembly of a bassinet.

"Not any more weird than inviting her to both my wedding and my baby shower," Maxine replied. "I know it's a bit unorthodox, but after Beau died when Hunter was two, we were the only family Cessy had left. Plus, Cooper won't admit it, but he secretly gets a real kick out of her."

Molly shook her head in doubt. "One of the blessings of calling off my wedding with Trevor was the knowledge that I'd never have to go to another luncheon with his mom again. Yes, she was actually stuck-up enough to call them 'luncheons.'"

Maxine nodded her head in Kaleb's direction. "Looks like that's not the only blessing to come out of your breakup."

Yeah, except it was tough to get too optimistic about another relationship that would be ending in a few days. Of course, since she couldn't correct her sister's—and everyone else in town's—assumption she changed the subject. "Do you know what this top secret plan of Hunter's is?"

"No clue," Maxine admitted. "He used to tell me everything but he's getting to that age. You know how it goes."

"How would I know how that goes?" Molly asked. "I don't have kids of my own, remember? Your friend Elaine was such a dear to bring that subject up in front of everyone today."

"Whoa." Maxine held up her pot holder–covered

hand. "First of all, I meant because you became the same way when you were Hunter's age. Second of all, Elaine is not my friend."

Before Molly could ask Maxine to expand on her initial statement, Cessy pulled out one of the counter stools and joined them. "Max, I told you I was sorry for inviting her. I was at the clerk's office in city hall talking to Mae Johnston about the shower cake we ordered from that fancy bakery in Boise. How was I supposed to know that Elaine was in line to get a permit for the remodel of the Gas N' Mart?"

"It's not your fault." Maxine squeezed the woman's shoulder. "Mia accidentally mentioned it at her yoga class last week, as well. Besides, it's a small town and Hunter is friends with her son."

"At least she brought a nice gift." Cessy poured herself another glass of wine, then extended the bottle.

"No, thanks." Molly took a big gulp of her water. "So did you like all your presents?"

"Oh, my gosh!" Maxine squealed. "I meant to tell you, that crib mattress you got me was so perfect. I got rid of Hunter's when he was a toddler because I didn't think I'd ever have another kid. When I found out I was pregnant, one of the ladies who works at the cookie shop gave me her daughter's old one. It was in great condition, but when we got it home, the mattress had all these yellow stains and it reminded me of that hand-me-down bed we got from Tommy."

Molly pointed at her sister. "That was my exact same thought when I saw them in the store."

Maxine laughed, then said, "Remember when he would babysit us, then put a cheap frozen pizza in the oven and force us watch that Tom Cruise movie so we'd leave him and his girlfriend alone while they made out on the back porch? We should've told her about his bedwetting problem. That would've put an end to his romantic endeavors."

"I loved those pizzas!" Molly put her hand to her heart.

"Too bad I can only provide you with the good stuff from Patrelli's tonight." Maxine opened the oven and the scent of garlic and pepperoni was like a punch in the gut since Molly knew she would have to limit herself to just one slice. "But we can ask the guys to find *Top Gun* on Netflix."

"I wish I would've had a sister," Cessy said. "You two are so lucky to have each other."

Were they? Molly had never thought about what it would be like to be an only child. Sure, there were times growing up when she probably wished that she could have something new or have more of her parents' attention, but she'd never resented her brothers and sister. She'd also never appreciated them, either. They were just there. She had no other basis for comparison until she'd met the Chattersons and caught a glimpse of what she'd been missing.

Suddenly, it felt like the most important thing in the world was to connect with her sister. To make up for lost time.

"Is dinner ready yet?" Hunter asked, a crumpled set of instructions in his hand. "We need to take a break from bassinet building."

"But I've almost figured out what we're supposed to do with the rocker base," Kaleb called out from behind the screen of his phone where he was probably watching a how-to video.

As Molly and Cessy carried the food to the wooden farmhouse table in the dining room, Cooper gently massaged Maxine's lower back and told her she should sit down and put her feet up. How sweet was it that her sister had found a man who was so caring and always concerned for her well-being.

"Do you want me to grab your meter for you before we eat?" Kaleb whispered from behind her shoulder. Huh. For some reason, it didn't sound as sweet and caring when Kaleb did it. It sounded bossy.

"I already did." When his eyebrow didn't go down, she sighed. "It's at eighty-eight."

"You're perfect," he said, then kissed her cheek. "And that's a pretty good number, too."

Maybe it was all the baby talk and childhood memories and lovey-dovey affection between all the couples in this town, but Kaleb's compliment made her glow. Or maybe her brain was still baffled by how he never needed to look at the miniature chart she carried around with her as a cheat sheet of what her levels were supposed to be.

"Aunt Molly, come sit on this side of the table by Gram," Hunter said, holding out a chair. "I want to be next to Kaleb when we tell you so we can both see your excitement."

Great. She got to be the center of attention when all she'd wanted to do today was hide out. Expectation crackled in the air. This better be something good. Otherwise, she couldn't promise that her reaction wouldn't disappoint them.

Everyone began passing food and Molly told herself that she could have just a couple of garlic knots. She'd been so good with all those stupid salads lately. When the last platter had been set down, Hunter used his fork and knife to drumroll the table.

"So your nephew came up—" Kaleb started.

"No, let me tell her," Hunter interrupted. "So, I was asking Kaleb about what games his company was working on next, and he said that when you guys were at Shadowview the other day, he thought about creating some training simulators for wounded soldiers who might feel like they're missing out on the action."

"What were you doing at Shadowview, Molly?" Maxine paused midbite. Everyone turned to stare, and the feeling made her want to jump out of her chair and run out of the house. Or sob out a confession. It would've been a good time to come clean if Cessy wasn't sitting beside her, absorbing every word quicker than she was absorbing the pinot noir. Plus, the use of the term *wounded soldiers* ruffled the hairs on the back of her neck. She didn't know where this was going, but she certainly wasn't wounded.

"Just some routine tests and stuff," Molly answered before shoving a bite of sausage and mushroom pizza into her mouth.

"Anyway, we were talking about how cool it would be to make flight simulators that make people feel like they're sitting in a cockpit. Or even a tank. We could do tanks, too, right, Kaleb? Hey, what about submarines? That would be so sweet!"

"Sure," Kaleb replied, his fingers steepled under his chin and his eyes dialed in on Molly as if her opinion was the most important thing in the room. The problem was, she didn't know what her opinion was.

"Uh-huh," Molly said since everyone was clearly waiting for a response. "And this would relate to me how?"

"Kaleb would hire you on as a consultant to help him design everything for the jet ones." Hunter's grin grew wide, but Molly's rib cage seemed to narrow. "Like a real job. He'd pay you and everything. Do you know how much money software developers make at his company?"

Kaleb's face suddenly swiveled to look at Hunter and she would've laughed at the surprise on his face if she wasn't trying to process what exactly was happening. "How do you know how much my employees make?"

"But, sweetie." Maxine brushed her hand over Hunter's hair, preventing him from incriminating himself. "Aunt Molly already has a job. When you're in the military, you can't just take off for a better paying gig."

Cooper didn't say a word, but his look spoke volumes. Molly fired back at her brother-in-law's silent chastisement with a sharp but subtle nod toward Cessy. She really didn't want to have this conversation right now with so many witnesses.

While Molly couldn't deny her curiosity at the idea, any potential excitement stirring to life in her belly was easily doused by the threat of Maxine learning the truth. She was already dreading the time when she would have to make a decision about her career, Molly didn't want to think about her limited choices in front of an audience. And she especially didn't want to think about the fact that her nephew and her nonboyfriend had gone ahead and mapped out her future—over a round of golf, no less—without even bothering to consult her.

## Chapter Fourteen

Kaleb took one look at Molly's expression and sat up straight in his dining room chair, realizing that he had to reassure her that he wasn't blowing her cover.

"You wouldn't need to leave your job. Unless, you know, you wanted to." Kaleb was quick to hedge his bets. "With all of our technology, we could do a lot of the work via emails and video conferences and what not. In fact, you wouldn't necessarily need to be there in person. A lot of it would be, uh, advisory."

"Well, I think that's a fabulous idea, you two." Cessy clapped twice, making a row of gold bracelets jingle along her wrist. "What can I do to help?"

"Um, what do you mean?" Kaleb looked across the table. Who was this woman again? Maxine's mother-in-law? Or former mother-in-law? He wished he hadn't been so quick to throw out his life preserver to Molly because he had a sudden premonition that *he* was the one who would need to be saved after this dinner.

"What about interior decorating? I could do that," Cessy suggested. "I mean, obviously you're going to need someone to pick out the leather for the cockpit chair or design where all those blinking lights go inside the submarine. Do they have beds in tanks? Because we could do some darling coverlets that incorporate a camouflage theme. Ooh, we could probably come up with some very neutral color schemes to appeal to people who aren't into all that military stuff."

"Why would someone not into military stuff want to drive a tank?" Maxine asked.

"It wouldn't be a life-size tank," Kaleb clarified. "Just a simulator of one. Really, we only came up with the idea this afternoon. It's not actually in the works. Yet."

"But he'll do it," Hunter assured everyone at the table, including Kaleb, who still had more than his share of doubts. "I watched that interview on *60 Minutes* when you told Lesley Stahl that once you visualize an idea, you always see it through to completion."

Kaleb shrugged. "Yeah, but my visualization process is pretty in-depth and—"

"I already drew up some designs." Hunter stood up. "I'll go grab them so we can get the ball rolling."

Molly rubbed at her temples before sneaking a sip of wine from Cessy's glass. Kaleb should probably ask her to step outside so they could—

"Ohhhh," Maxine moaned as she grabbed her stomach and her husband sent his chair flying backward.

"Are you okay?" Molly asked her sister.

Cooper's face grew pale. "I think it's time."

\* \* \*

Kaleb had never been more thankful to have a woman go into labor than he was at that second. Maxine and Cooper left for the hospital while Cessy and Hunter quickly packed up a bag of everything they thought she would need and followed in a separate car.

Molly volunteered the two of them to clean up the dishes and put the food away. Because she had already been on edge before, Kaleb didn't say a word until the kitchen was spotless.

When there was nothing left to do but start the dishwasher, he asked, "Do you want me to drive you to the hospital?"

"I don't know," Molly replied. "I probably should wait to hear something from Cooper. What if it's a false alarm or something?"

"Should we stay here?"

"I don't know," Molly repeated. Kaleb's muscles twitched, anxious to do something. To make some sort of decision.

"I'll tell you what. Why don't we head down there? If they send her home, then we come back. But sitting around and waiting is going to make us nuts."

"Us? Or you?"

He rolled his eyes. "Us, because I'll eventually get so stir-crazy that I'll get on your nerves."

"Fine." She grabbed her purse and they locked up the house. When they climbed inside the truck, she added, "You don't have to drive me all the way down there, though. Just drop me off at the apartment and I can take my own car."

He tried to ignore the uncertainty settling on his

chest. He hated being unsure of something even more than he hated waiting. "You don't want me to take you?"

"I've seen how you get in hospitals."

"Well, I've seen how you get behind the wheel. I think we'll all be safer if I drive."

"If you think I'm such a bad driver, why would you create some sympathy pilot consultation job for me?"

Aha! He *knew* she was annoyed by that. But he didn't understand why until she'd implied that he'd only done it out of pity. "Actually, Hunter was the one who suggested that you'd be good at it."

"So you're not really offering me the job?"

"Is there a way for me to answer this question without you being pissed off at me?"

"Probably not." It was too dark inside the cab of the truck to see her face so he couldn't tell if she was joking. "Is this really something you're planning or was it just something you went along with to appease my nephew? Like that summer internship you promised him?"

"When it comes to my company, I don't appease anyone."

"Hmm." She shifted in her seat. Kaleb sensed her studying him and he wondered if her ex had made her mistrustful of all men. "So this is seriously something you're considering doing?"

"I've wanted to get into a project bigger than video games for a while now, but I hadn't been able to figure out what. My roommate from college is designing robotic lasers that can perform complicated surgeries, and one of our classmates invented photovoltaic software for solar panels. Other people in my industry are coming up with self-driving cars and technology that nobody had even dreamed about five years ago. And I sell computer-animated worlds where people can craft things with blocks, or pretend they're a sports MVP, or force aliens and pirates and zombies to fight for control over the galaxy. When we were at Shadowview, that bald guy made a point about how the video games they were playing weren't doing anything to benefit them or benefit the world."

"Really? Because I watched those other patients playing your games and you brought them joy," Molly argued.

"I used to think that, too. Yet, lately I'm wondering if that's enough."

"Kaleb, sometimes people need an escape from the real world and you've been able to provide that. That man in the cast was working on his own demons and you can't take it personally. You can't solve everybody's problems."

Yet, that's what Kaleb did. He invented, he developed, he solved. His family, and even Molly, had made enough pointed comments over the week to make him question whether he was really the corporate genius and a successful entrepreneur he thought he'd become. So Kaleb didn't admit that the soldier wasn't the only one who'd brought his attention to some deep-seated inadequacy he hadn't known existed.

"He also dissed my T-shirt," he complained.

Molly laughed. "For the record, I like the way you dress. Could you imagine how unapproachable you'd be if you wore fancy suits?"

"What do you mean unapproachable?" he asked, hating that he was fishing for affirmation.

"You're this billionaire, hotshot, computer whiz. Kids want to be you when they grow up. Do you know how many people would kill for your intelligence or for even a quarter of your fortune? And if that's not unfair enough, you're always the most handsome man in the room."

"Will you tell Kane that I'm the most handsome man in the room and tell Kylie that you like my character shirts?"

"No way. Watching your family tease you also makes you more approachable. So don't worry." She reached across the center console and squeezed his leg. "In a couple of days you can go back to your old life and be as powerful and superior as you like."

Right. So then why did that sound like a punishment?

## *Chapter Fifteen*

Sunday was the day of the Sun Potato Parade and Festival, not to be confused with the Ski Potato Parade and Festival, which took place in the winter. Kaleb woke up in Molly's bed that morning knowing that tomorrow would be their last day together. He studied her sleeping form curled against his side. Her tan skin soft and warm, her blond curls tangled and sexy.

Last night, just before they turned onto the highway to go into Boise, Cooper had sent Molly a text saying it wasn't actual labor, only something called Braxton-Hicks contractions, and they were sending Maxine home.

So Kaleb had turned around and driven them back to the apartment. He knew Molly was emotionally drained so it hadn't surprised him when she'd fallen asleep before they returned. What had surprised him was that she'd dozed off with her smartphone in her hand, the screen still lit up with results from her internet search of "pregnancy and type 1 diabetes."

He'd never thought about having kids, but it broke his heart to think that she might want children and wouldn't be able to have one of her own. When he parked in the alley behind the cookie shop, he let Molly sleep in the seat beside him as he used his own phone to do some research. He was relieved to find out that while it could be risky, it was still possible.

Then he'd tried to be romantic and lifted her out of the passenger side of the truck to carry her up the stairs to the apartment. But she woke up and drowsily commanded him to put her down before he hurt his back.

They'd made love only once last night, and even though they'd used protection, Kaleb couldn't stop thinking about the possibility of having a child with her. Kids had never really been on his radar before. There were just so many other things he'd envisioned doing with his life first. But if he was going to have a son or daughter, he would want them to have a mother as strong and as courageous as Molly. As he held her close and drifted off to sleep, the idea of fatherhood didn't seem quite so far-fetched.

Waking up, all the baby thoughts began to permeate his mind again, just like the sun pushing itself through closed wooden shutters. He tried to shut them out. To tell himself that by this time next year, he'd be a distant memory for her and she'd be the punch line of an embarrassing story his brothers told about him. *Hey, you guys remember that time Kaleb fell for the sexy combat pilot and she shot him down?*

He knew she'd said that she wasn't looking for a

relationship because she had her future to figure out. Kaleb hadn't been looking for one, either. He'd never had to. Back in high school and college, he'd learned early on that the only girls who were interested in him cared more about his family's money and his famous last name. And those weren't the type of girls hanging out in the video game lounge at the student center or in the computer store, where Kaleb tended to spend most of his time. When he'd started Perfect Game Industries after his junior year, he was so busy launching his company, there wasn't any spare time to eat, let alone date.

The more successful he became, the more people wanted something from him, the more he was invited to attend lavish social events. He hated going, but he knew that he was the face of his corporation, and as much as he wanted to, he couldn't hide behind his laptop all the time. Then, the more social events he attended, the more women threw themselves at him.

But no matter how much money he made, Kaleb remained the same person. The same shy, geek who would rather go to the office than go to parties. Which only cemented the fact that women who wouldn't normally give a guy like him the time of day, were only doing so because of the perks that came with dating a famous billionaire.

If he needed a date to walk the red carpet of a premiere or to be his plus one whenever he was the guest of honor at some convention, there was always one willing to escort him. Usually, they were equally willing to stay the night with him afterward if he was in the mood. Most were comfortable with the arrangement, but every once in a while, he'd date a woman who expected something more and he'd have to ask Angela to send a bouquet and his apologies. He'd never understood those expectations.

Until now.

Kaleb had formed some sort of attachment to Molly this past week and he wasn't quite ready to move on. A few days ago, it would've been easy to tell himself that after he returned to work and fully immersed himself back into the business, his feelings toward her would eventually cool. But what if they didn't?

Molly was unlike any of the women he'd dated in the past. She wasn't impressed with his company or his money or what he could do for her. In fact, he got the feeling that she would probably like him more if he was just an average guy with average resources. Perhaps he was simply suffering from a case of wanting what he couldn't have.

And right this second, there was no denying that he wanted her.

Currently, she was sleeping soundly with her knee hitched across his thighs and he couldn't bring himself to untangle his body from hers long enough to use the restroom. How in the world was he going to go back to Seattle without her?

He could try to return to work, waiting and biding his time until she finally figured out what she needed. However, he'd had enough waiting in hospital rooms and traction beds and back braces while his teenage years had passed him by. Clearly, she was holding out hope of returning to the military but he'd done plenty of research lately and the writing was on the wall. Molly had a doctor's appointment tomorrow and he was pretty sure that they were going to confirm her medical discharge. So it seemed clear to him that the best path for

her was to come and work for his company as a consultant.

Kaleb stared up at the ceiling, plotting the best way
to get her to come to that decision on her own. When
they'd told her about the flight simulator idea last night,
Molly hadn't seemed as excited about the prospect as
he would've hoped. But he had a feeling that was because she was more concerned with the fact that they'd
brought it up in front of Maxine and she was worried
that he'd let something slip.

They hadn't discussed salary, but only because he
doubted Molly was the type to be persuaded by the al-
mighty dollar. After all, she chose to be a military pilot
rather than a commercial one, which made it pretty clear
where her priorities were. Maybe he should appeal to
her sense of adventure?

Kaleb was used to giving orders and she'd been
trained to follow them—as long as they came from a
commanding officer and not from him. He was also
used to solving problems and she needed a solution.
He'd found the perfect one. All he needed to do today
was convince her that his plan was in her best interests.

Being careful not to wake her, he gently raised his
forearm up and reached over her sleeping head as he
typed out a text message on his watch.

Snowflake Boulevard was closed to traffic and the
last Miss Sun Potato contestant's float had just passed
Molly and Kaleb. The volunteer mounted rescue patrol—
which was actually only four people on horses—carried
the final banner that would close out the parade.

Two months ago, if someone had told Molly that she'd
be standing on the sidewalk of a small town wearing

a Styrofoam potato on her head and waving a miniature version of the Idaho flag at the local high school marching band, she would've doubled over in laughter. Yet, here she was on a sunny Sunday afternoon, Kaleb standing behind her with his arms wrapped around her waist, and her sister's family beside them.

It was a little too relaxed, a little too simple, a little too everything. And by tomorrow evening, it would all be over. Molly leaned against him, but resisted the urge to intertwine her fingers with his, to hold on to him a little longer.

She would be going to the doctor in the morning, and although she'd once held out hope, there was no longer a doubt in her mind that the news wouldn't be what she wanted to hear. Molly had no idea when Kaleb was planning to leave town, but his company jet was supposed to be picking him up tomorrow. As far as Mondays went, the upcoming one was promising to be pretty brutal.

Reminding herself that it wasn't like the world was going to crash down around her, she pasted a smile on her face and set out to have a perfect last day together. They walked along the vendor booths set up in the town square park and Molly was surprised by how many people said hello to them. More shocking was the fact that she actually knew at least half of their names. She wasn't convinced that small-town life was for her, but with all the uncertainties she was experiencing lately, there was definitely something comforting about the familiarity and the slower pace.

"You want a snow cone, Aunt Molly?" Hunter asked her.

"No way, buddy." She tugged on the bill of his baseball cap. "That's pure sugar."

"What about a funnel cake?" he asked. Molly spotted an older man with a toothpick hanging out of his mouth, carrying a plate of some sort of fried dough buried underneath a pile of canned cherry compote and whipped cream.

"I'll just have a bite of whatever you get," she told her nephew.

Kaleb, who was walking with his arm draped over her shoulders, used his hip to slightly bump her. "Check you out, making all the healthy choices."

"And I didn't even need you to boss me about it." She wrapped her hand around his waist. "I told you that I would eventually figure it out for myself."

But instead of returning her playful smile, he gave her an odd look. After a few more steps, he tried to steer her toward a booth with an enormous fabric sign that read Sugar Stitchers.

"Are you in the market for a new quilt?" she asked him with a sideways glance.

"Maybe. Do you know there's a whole niche of software programs for designing quilting patterns?"

"That's fascinating. And here, I thought you were trying to avoid running into all your brothers who are lined up over by the dunk tank."

"That, too." He kept his attention locked on to the sunflower pattern of a displayed blanket. "Are they taking bets yet?"

"I can't tell from here. But it looks like the mayor is coming down from the perch over the water and Kevin is taking his spot."

"In that case, things might actually get interesting."

Kaleb immediately switched directions and yelled over the crowd, "I get first pitch!"

As much as Molly wanted to watch the competition, her tote bag vibrated and she reached inside to pull out her phone. Looking at the screen, she gulped. "This is my commanding officer. I better take this."

Kaleb's face was completely expressionless. "Do you want me to stay with you?"

She tried to chuckle, but her mouth had already gone dry. "I'm sure I can handle a phone call by myself. Go play with your brothers, and if you dunk one of them, I'll buy you a corn dog."

"Hopefully, you'll have something to celebrate, too," he said with a smile before walking off.

That was an odd thing to say, Molly thought before she swiped her finger across the screen. "Hello, Sir."

"Markham," his gravelly voice barked out. "How's your leave going?"

"I'm currently at a potato festival in Idaho, so I'm not sure if that's a good thing or a bad thing, Sir."

"What have the doctors at Shadowview said?"

Nothing. Because she'd been putting off her appointment until tomorrow. She bit her lip before giving a mostly true answer. "We're waiting for some test results."

"I know the Bureau of Personnel isn't likely to give you your wings back, but I've got some good news. Someone must have pulled some strings for you because I just got a call from the Joint Staff Surgeon over at the Pentagon and they're willing to give you a desk assignment if you'll agree to serving as an adviser on a special training program they're coming up with."

*Pulled some strings for you?* His words sent off an alarm bell. "What kind of special training program?"

"I've never heard of it because it's still in the beginning stages. Something about flight simulators," he said, and Molly's blood went cold. "Anyway, they'll let you retain your rank and your pay scale. So unless the doctors tell you otherwise, it's either this new gig or a medical retirement."

"Thank you for calling, Sir." Her jaw was clenched so tightly it was a wonder she could say that much. "I'll let you know what I decide to do."

She disconnected and saw a haze of red as she stormed over to the dunk tank. Looking for Kaleb in the crowd, she narrowed her eyes when she spotted him sitting on the perch over the tank, laughing at something a soaking wet Bobby Junior said to him.

"Hey, Molly." Kevin, who was also drenched, handed her a baseball. "You want to give it a shot?"

"Whoa," Kaleb yelled from over the tank. "I thought the rules were Chattersons only. No bringing in a ringer."

Oh, she'd show him ringer. She squeezed the sewed seams on the ball until she thought it might burst as she yelled, "I just had a very interesting call with my commanding officer."

Kaleb's smirk fell. "Why don't I climb out of here and we can talk about it in private?"

"In private? Apparently, that's how you like to operate, isn't it, Kaleb? Behind the scenes? Like the wizard hiding in back of the curtain?" Molly didn't notice that the crowd had doubled in size or that the only sound now came from the Dixieland band in the gazebo on the other side of the park. "Well, then, let's just get it all out in the open."

"I've been waiting over a week for you to get things out in the open, Molly." He sent her a warning look, but it didn't faze her. She was beyond furious and she didn't care who knew.

"So all week you've been planning on creating some fake duty assignment for me out of pity? Poor Molly has diabetes and can't take care of herself. Have you been leading me on this whole time?"

"You have diabetes?" Maxine whispered, but Molly was too fired up to worry about her sister's reaction to the unexpected announcement of her diagnosis. This was between her and Kaleb. She'd deal with the fallout later.

"I never lied to you, Molly," Kaleb argued. "I told you that Hunter and I came up with that idea yesterday. You didn't seem to object, so I put out some feelers after that."

"Some feelers? You were able to call the Pentagon and send this down the chain of command on a Sunday morning!"

"I know some people who know some people. And I promised them a free prototype and a lowball bid."

"And what about me? What do I get out of this?"

"You get the chance to fly again, Molly!" He fired back.

Feeling an arm slip around her waist, she looked at Maxine, who was standing beside her—tall and pregnant and released from the hospital less than twenty-four hours ago, ready to do battle on her sister's behalf. Molly squared her shoulders, her sister silently giving her the strength to fight.

## Chapter Sixteen

Seeing the fury blazing in her eyes, Kaleb wanted to go back in time and delete that text asking Angela to email the Pentagon. Maybe he hadn't gone about it the right way, but he was still sure he'd done the right thing. He just needed to convince her—and her equally angry looking sister—that this was for the best.

"I'm sorry, Molly. I was only trying to—"

"This is my life, Kaleb. It's not a game!" she yelled at him before winding up and hurling the ball for the metal-plated target on the side of the tank.

Ding!

The freezing water shocked him and everything went blurry as the realization of what he'd just done numbed him. If he was Aquaman, he could stay in here forever and never deal with the damage he'd just caused. But he wasn't a superhero. He'd tried to act like one and save the day; however, all he'd done was screw things up. When he finally broke the surface and came up for air, he looked around for Molly, but she was gone.

Half the crowd was still there, though, including his three brothers and his dad, who was shoving fistfuls of popcorn into his mouth. Kevin reached his hand into the striped box but their father yanked it away.

"Go get your own," Bobby Senior said, then looked at Kaleb. "You gonna sit in the dunk tank all day or are you going to drag your dumb keister out of there and find the long-lost sense you were supposedly born with?"

Kaleb took plenty of teasing from his family, but it was rare when anyone accused him of not being smart. Yet, even he had to admit that he'd just pulled one of the most stupid moves ever.

It took a couple of tries to heave himself from the water because each time he would reach for the perch to haul himself up, one of his brothers would push the target-shaped lever, causing him to fall back in. He shot them all a ha-ha smile when he finally climbed over the Plexiglas side and plopped onto the grass outside the tank.

The early-evening mountain breeze had picked up and sent a shiver coursing through him, wiping away his short-lived triumph. "It's freezing out here."

Kane, Kevin and Bobby Junior were still damp from their own forays into the tank—one of their dunkings courtesy of Kaleb—so they gave him no sympathy. At least his old man was able to muster up some pity. "Come on, son. Let's get you warmed up. Then we can talk about this mess you got yourself into."

Kaleb didn't exactly want to talk about anything with anyone except Molly. "Do you know where she went?"

"I know where she *didn't* go." His dad firmly patted him on the back, propelling him across the midway. "To get you a towel."

The breeze picked up, reminding Kaleb that it might be best to dry off before he went looking for her. Molly wasn't the type of woman who would care about his appearance, but if he was going to go begging for forgiveness, he didn't want to resemble a drowned rat. The three hundred-dollar bills he pulled from his waterlogged wallet were still dripping when he exchanged them for a homemade quilt at the Sugar Stitchers booth.

The cookie shop was only a few blocks from the park, so he turned to head there first. Until his dad put a beefy hand on Kaleb's shoulder.

"Hold up, kiddo. Let her cool off a little." Bobby Chatterson hadn't called him "kiddo" since his final spine fusion surgery. That meant his dad thought the situation was pretty serious. "Let's grab a seat. It wouldn't kill you to learn a little patience."

As much as he wanted to race after Molly, perhaps now wasn't the time to rush into things if he didn't have a strategy in place. And Coach Chatterson prided himself on being a master strategist. Kaleb had his doubts, but settled in next to his father, anyway. "You know, the last time I sat next to you in a park with a blanket wrapped around me, I was twelve and had just been released from the hospital before Kane's Little League tournament."

"Huh." His dad nodded. "I remember your mom insisted that you stay home with her but you called old Mrs. Kenmore across the street and asked her to babysit you so that your mother wouldn't miss the playoff game. Then you snuck into the back of the car and covered up with that old fleece throw. You really pissed your momma off with that stunt."

"But it worked. The babysitter never even knew I was gone because I'd built that humanoid robot, stuffed it under my covers and programmed it to switch positions every thirty minutes. And I got to stay and watch the game with everyone else."

"Stay and watch the game?" His dad gave him an incredulous look. "Kaleb, you only lasted through the second inning because those metal bleachers were hell on your spine after that surgery. I had to drive you home while you laid there all stiff like a mummy in the back seat. It added a whole month onto your physical therapy regime. I sold that stupid robot to the scrap yard and poor Mrs. Kenmore refused to ever babysit any of you again after that."

"I'm pretty sure she refused after Kevin turned the hose on her the same day her daughter gave her a home permanent."

"My point, son—" Bobby Chatterson waited until he had Kaleb's full attention "—is that even the best-laid plans can result in consequences. And I have a feeling that this stunt you pulled on Molly today wasn't well laid at all."

"It wasn't a stunt, Dad. I was actually trying to help her."

"By getting her commanding officer to order her to come and work for you? Trust me, ladies don't like it when you interfere with their careers."

Oh, please. His dad was the biggest interferer of all the Chattersons.

"That's not exactly the way it went down." Kaleb looked at all the people still lingering in the town square and partaking of the festivities. Not that it mattered who overheard them at this point. Most of them had already heard Molly inadvertently announce her secret to the world. "A few weeks ago, she found out she had type 1 diabetes, which is an immediate disqualification for having a pilot's license."

"That diabetes is nasty stuff. My doctor told me I had the same thing. Put me on some pills and now I'm good as new."

Kaleb stared at his father's heavier frame. Like three of his sons, Bobby Chatterson had also been a professional baseball pitcher, but he'd stopped running the bases—or running anywhere—after he became a coach. "Actually, Dad, you have type 2, which is a lot different than type 1. Molly can't regulate it with a pill or with diet alone. She has to carry around insulin and constantly check her blood sugar levels because she's always at risk for an attack."

His dad frowned. "Kane's right. You really are a know-it-all."

"Do you want to hear this or not?"

"Carry on."

"The type 1 diagnosis also automatically makes her ineligible for service because she's not fit for duty."

"But she's perfectly fit!" his dad argued, and Kaleb thought, *You have no idea.*

"Right. But it's still a military regulation that she be 'operational ready' at all times, whatever that means. As a combat pilot, it's common for them to go on training missions for twenty-four to forty-eight hours straight. And with her body requiring constant monitoring, along with needing food and insulin doses on a certain schedule, they can't take that risk. So her flight surgeon wrote up a medical board, which is this big file documenting her condition and the lab findings. She can fight it on an appeal, but basically it's a losing battle. Right now, she's in a holding pattern until she goes before the Bureau of Personnel and they determine how much of her base pay she'll be awarded for a medical discharge."

"Damn shame," his father muttered, and Kaleb had to agree.

"I know how much she loves being a pilot and how much the Air Force means to her. Plus, I'd been toying with the idea of designing some flight simulators—" okay, so really, he'd only been toying with the idea for twenty-four hours, but his dad didn't need to know that "—and thought she'd make a perfect consultant. I called up someone I knew in the Pentagon who owed me a favor—"

"Hold up. You have contacts in the Pentagon who owe you favors?" his dad asked in a hushed voice, then waved his hand. "Never mind. We'll talk about that later."

"Anyway, I think you and the rest of the town know about her commanding officer calling her and the job assignment and all the rest. But really, Dad, it's a foolproof solution to her problem."

"Except you're forgetting one little thing."

"What's that?"

"Molly Markham is no fool."

Kaleb threw his head back. "Nobody knows that better than me, Dad."

"Really? Because I'm having a hard time believing that. You're an independent guy, right? You pride yourself on the fact that you never followed in my or your brothers' footsteps and played ball."

"Uh, because I couldn't, Dad. Remember my back

surgeries? Remember your and mom's rule about no contact sports?"

"Meh. Since when did we ever enforce any rules at our house? Sure, we would've been scared to death to let you play, but you could've gotten us to back down. Just like you did when you hid in the car and talked us into letting you watch Kane's game. You never pushed because you weren't passionate about sports. You preferred computers and gaming and that was what you were good at. So you built your career the way you wanted it."

"What do you mean you would've backed down? Are you saying that all this time I could've played baseball if I'd wanted to?"

"Son, if you could leave your company today and become the starting pitcher for a major league team, would you do it?"

"Depends on which team," Kaleb murmured, knowing there was no way he'd play for the one his old man coached.

His dad cupped his ear. "What's that?"

"I guess not," Kaleb admitted.

"See, you chose your own path and it was the right one for you. Now, here's what you're going to do. Give Molly some time to cool down. Then you go talk to her. Tell her what a dumbass you were and how you'll never meddle in her life again."

"How do you know that'll work?"

"Because that's what I did when I made the same mistake with your mom. And we're going on thirty-five years next month."

"I think I'm afraid to ask for details on how you interfered in Mom's life."

"Oh, she had it in her head that she wanted to be an interior decorator. She was even in this special school for it and everything. But then I got her knocked up with Bobby Junior."

"Yeah, but that could've happened to any... Oh, geez, Dad, you did it on purpose?"

"No, not on purpose," his father snapped. "But I did spill the beans to your grandad and he told us in no uncertain terms that there wouldn't be a long engagement. Besides, she went back and got her degree and I've given her plenty of houses to decorate over the years. My point is that I apologized, even though I wasn't really all that sorry."

"So you think Molly will forgive me?"

"Does she love you?"

He thought about her speech the morning after they'd first slept together. She was clear that she wasn't looking for anything serious because she needed to figure her life out. Kaleb had merely been trying to hurry the process along. It didn't occur to him that she might not share his feelings because until this morning, he didn't even know what his own feelings were. "We've only known each other for a little over a week."

"Do you love her?"

"I don't know," Kaleb said, then sneezed. His head pounded.

"Well, this isn't something you can ask your assistant or the Pentagon about. Only you can solve that one. I know you're used to getting instant answers, but relationships take time."

Kaleb's only response was to sneeze again.

"C'mon. Let's get you home. Your mother's going to kill me if I let you catch pneumonia."

As they walked to his dad's truck, Kaleb asked, "How long do you think it'll take?"

"To know whether or not you love her?" His father draped an arm over his shoulder. "Kiddo, if you don't already know, you will by tomorrow morning. You've never been able to wait for nothin'."

Molly's heart leaped when a knock sounded on the apartment door late that evening. She grabbed a paper towel from the kitchen and used it to scrub the tears off her face before she unlocked the dead bolt.

But it wasn't Kaleb on the other side.

"Do you mind if I come in?" Maxine asked.

"It's your apartment," Molly said, standing aside.

"Do you want to talk about it?"

"Not really."

Her sister waddled over to the sofa and collapsed on the cushions. "Then I'll just wait here until you do."

And because stubbornness ran in the Markham blood, Molly sighed and took the armchair across from her. "I'm sorry I didn't tell you what was going on sooner. But I was dealing with a lot of new feelings and uncertainties."

"When you took off from the festival, I wanted to run after you. I would've been here sooner if I had. But we've never been the kind of sisters who tell each other everything and I decided that I should try to get as much information as I could before I offer to give you any advice."

"So you stayed and talked to Kaleb?" Molly asked.

"No. I went over to the police station and Cooper let me use his laptop. I researched type 1 diabetes."

"Why does everyone do that?"

"Didn't you?"

"No. I was too busy looking up every other possible disease it could have been. I was hoping for a misdiagnosis."

"One of the online articles I read was that it can feel like a very lonely condition."

"Well, I'm used to being alone."

"You don't have to be," Maxine said, pushing a strand of hair behind Molly's ear. "Why didn't you tell me?"

"I was going to. But I wanted to do it in my own way."

"In front of the whole town at the Sun Potato Festival?"

Molly dipped her head in shame. "No. But I was so mad at Kaleb, it just came flying out of my mouth before I could stop it. I'm sorry you had to find out that way."

"Well, at least I finally found out," Maxine leaned her head back and let out a sigh. "I had a feeling something was up, but I didn't know what to do or how to help."

"That's why I didn't say anything because I didn't want you worrying about me."

"I'm your big sister. Even when we're not together, I still worry about you."

"I'm sorry for keeping it a secret." Molly's heart expanded and she squeezed her sister's hand. "I've always taken care of myself, done things on my own. Then when I came to Sugar Falls, I was forced to confront the fact that I was no longer in control of everything. But now that you know—along with everyone else in this small town—I already feel like a huge weight's been lifted off of me."

"I'm glad you're here, Moll Doll. I want you to know that I'm here for you, too. Whatever you need emotionally, medically, heck, even nutritionally. I already make gluten free cookies at the shop. I'm sure I can come up with some sugar free ones, too."

Molly held up her hand. "See? Now that you know, you're babying me. I don't want people treating me like I'm going to fall apart if I eat a baked good. I'm going to mess up and get my levels wrong and make mistakes. It's now obvious that I'm going to need some support, but I also have to figure things out on my own."

"Fine. I'll try not to be supportive without going into overprotective mode and smothering you with my concern."

"Good. Because I've gotten more than enough of that from Kaleb. He always thinks he knows what's best."

"It's obvious that he cares about you."

"I don't really want to talk about him," Molly murmured. She'd already said too much in front of too many people and her emotional well was running dry.

"Okay." Her sister paused before switching tactics. "So what's going to happen to your career?"

"I really don't want to talk about that, either."

"Then what do you want to talk about?"

"I don't want to talk. I just want to go to sleep."

"That's another thing I read when I was researching. That sometimes you'll get tired for no reason at all. Have you been sleeping okay?"

The truth was, with Kaleb spending the past three nights, neither one of them had gotten much sleep at all. Instead of replying, she yawned.

"Fine, then we'll go to bed," Maxine said. "We can talk about everything in the morning."

But when Molly stood up to walk down the hall, her sister followed. "Don't you need to get home?"

"Nope. I told Cooper I was going to stay with you tonight."

"You really don't have to do that."

"I know."

"When it comes to being overprotective, you might actually be worse than Kaleb," Molly said as she began to arrange pillows on the bed.

"So then you *do* want to talk about him?"

She shot Maxine an annoyed look, but really, she was glad her sister was here. For the first time in her life, she didn't want to be alone. They didn't say another word, and in the morning, Molly was surprised to see her sister sound asleep on top of the covers.

"What are you still doing here?" she asked when Maxine finally opened her eyes.

"Sleeping. It's not like it's the first time we've had to share a bed."

Molly rolled her eyes. "But it's the first time you were almost nine months pregnant and snored the whole night."

"I don't snore."

"How sweet that your husband lets you believe that."

Maxine swacked her with a pillow. "So what are you going to do about Kaleb?"

"There's nothing to do. He's going back to Seattle today and I don't know where I'm going. Or what I'm going to do when I get there."

"Have you thought about taking his job offer?"

"Of course I have! It would probably be the next best thing to flying. But I can't stand the fact that he came up with it as a way to micromanage my life."

"Do you think you're being a little stubborn?" It took a couple of tries for Maxine to heft herself up into a sitting position. "What does it matter whose idea it was? If it's a good one, you should jump all over it."

"But what if I actually had to work with him? I don't think I could handle that."

"Because you love him?"

Molly squeezed her eyes shut. "Maybe."

"Then it's worth a shot."

"You don't understand. This whole dating thing? It wasn't even real." Heck, if she was going to open up with her sister, she might as well tell her everything. "It was all for show to keep people from finding out about my condition."

"People or me?"

She wished she could wipe the injured look from her sister's face. "Mostly people. Because they would end up telling you. I needed time."

"So you guys weren't really involved romantically?"

"We were, but…it's complex."

"Then try to simplify it."

"We were supposed to only be going on platonic dates."

"What in the world is a platonic date?"

"Like enough of a date to make it look like he wasn't lying to his family outright, but not so serious that we would develop actual feelings for each other."

"It's nice that someone in the relationship didn't want to lie to their siblings," Maxine mumbled.

"It wasn't a lie. I said last night that I was just waiting to tell you. Even Cooper knew that."

"Wait, my husband found out about this but didn't tell me?"

"Not exactly." Molly cringed. How had she let the web spin so far out of control? "Remember how he and Hunter ran into us at Shadowview after I was getting some blood work done? Well, he kind of guessed that something was up, but didn't want to be responsible with knowing the details. I promised him that I would tell you after my appointment today. He said that if I didn't, he would."

"Did Hunter know about it, too?"

"No. At least, I'm pretty sure he didn't. Although sometimes it surprises me what that kid can find out."

"Okay, so back to the platonic dating," Maxine said. "How platonic are we talking about?"

Molly's cheeks burned. "Uh, pretty unplatonic."

"Did you guys…" Maxine swirled her fingers in a circle.

Molly hesitated. She was finally opening up and she wanted to continue sharing, but she was unsure of how much she should say. "Let's just say that things progressed way past the kissing stage and emotions got involved. At least, they did for me."

"But not for him?"

"Who can tell? He thinks about things down to the last detail. Everything is a game or a strategy for him. It's like being stuck in a perpetual chess match and I've only been given the rules for checkers."

"How did he benefit from this so-called game?"

"I don't know. He got to avoid his family, I guess."

"Oh, come on." Maxine flung her palm out. "Nobody buys that excuse. You've met the Chattersons. Who in their right mind would avoid that hilarious mess? They're dysfunctionally perfect. And no matter how much he says otherwise, the man adores them. I've been friends with Kylie for over ten years and Kaleb's never missed a family vacation. Four summers ago, he threw his parents a humongous thirtieth anniversary bash on some buddy's island off the coast of Bora-Bora. Those guys all act like they can't stand each other, but really, they thrive off each other. So since we can rule that out, why else would he insist on platonically dating you?"

Molly shrugged. "I guess he did it to keep my secret."

"Then you're just as big of a game player as him."

"How am I playing games?" she huffed.

"You said it yourself. You were trying to keep your diabetes a secret. From you own sister, no less," Maxine attempted a look of chastisement. "But what did Kaleb gain from this arrangement?"

"He got to boss me around?" Molly asked.

Maxine made a loud buzzer sound. "Try again."

All Molly could do was shrug.

"I've seen the way he looks at you," her sister continued. "And a man doesn't call in a favor to the Pentagon and create brand new flight simulator technology for a woman unless he cares about her."

"But Kaleb said he's not the serious relationship type."

"Would you be if you thought most of the women throwing themselves at you were only interested in your money and your famous name?"

"I guess not. But surely he knows that I don't care about any of that stuff."

"Of course he does." Maxine shot her a smug grin. "That's why he's doing everything in his power not to let you go."

## Chapter Seventeen

Kaleb had tossed and turned on his sister's sofa all night. He finally fell asleep at five o'clock and woke up to the smell of frozen waffles burning in the toaster. The battery on his smartwatch had died, so he sat up and turned to Kylie, who was fanning at the smoke in the kitchen.

"What time is it?" he asked.

"It's time you go find Molly and apologize for being such a dumbass yesterday."

"You know, I'm not exactly a fan of these new nicknames everyone's giving me. Whatever happened to Brainiac?" Kaleb, who'd slept in a pair of sweatpants he'd borrowed from his brother-in-law, pulled on a T-shirt.

"When you start acting like you have a brain, then maybe we'll start using it again." She poured coffee into a travel mug and held it out to him.

"Your waffles are burning again."

"Damn," she said as he headed to the restroom.

Ten minutes later, he was in the truck, scrolling through the recent destinations list until he found the address for Shadowview. Molly's appointment was for eight o'clock and it was now thirty minutes after that. Okay, so maybe he didn't need the GPS to tell him how to get there when he'd driven to the same place only a couple of days ago. But he was hoping to find a shorter route.

First his watch battery died and he'd slept through his alarm, and now this digital map on his dashboard was reminding him that there was only one road going in or out of Sugar Falls. Molly's past comments mocking his dependence on technology were coming back to haunt him.

Luckily, rush hour traffic through downtown was minimal and he quickly breezed through the city's four major stoplights. Unfortunately, he got stuck behind a tractor trailer slowly meandering down the highway, hauling one of the parade floats from yesterday. He eased across the yellow stripes, only to swerve back into place when he saw a lumbering RV steaming up the opposing lane, a line of cars trailing behind.

Molly probably would've gunned the engine and gone for it, but Kaleb wasn't that desperate. Yet. He used the radio controls embedded into the steering wheel to shuffle through his playlist, and when he couldn't find a song he liked, he switched off the radio. He hooked his Bluetooth headset onto his ear, then realized there was nobody he wanted to talk to but her. His watch, which was plugged into the charger in the center console, was finally at 20 percent so he switched it on to see if he'd missed a text from her.

He'd only been looking down for a second when one of the lengths of tinsel streamers from the float in front of him ripped off and landed on his windshield. He yanked the steering wheel to the right, applying the brake. However, he didn't see the object in the road until it was too late. The bounce jarred him as he thumped over it, then there was a loud bang before the rear of the vehicle began to shimmy.

Rolling down the window, he stuck his head out to watch for oncoming traffic as he hugged the shoulder of the road. Thankfully, there was a turnout ahead and he eased the truck off the highway.

Kaleb jumped out, yanking the streamer off his windshield and tossing it inside the cab before walking around to the back. A scrap of torn metal was completely embedded in the right rear tire. He lifted his head to the sky wondering if the universe was trying to send him some sort of signal.

Getting back in the truck, he pulled up his location on the GPS. His initial instinct was to call Angela and ask her to route a roadside assistance company to him. But he knew that all the money in the world wouldn't guarantee the response time he needed way out here on the mountain.

He'd already forced himself to wait more than twelve hours to go after Molly. Yet, now that he was finally so close, his patience was being tested again. But this time, he would take his time and he would do things himself—without the help of technology or assistants. Like his father had told him last night, when he wanted something badly enough, he didn't give up. Kaleb needed to prove it to himself before he could prove it to her.

The white paper liner crackled and ripped as Molly climbed down from the exam table in the endocrinologist's office. The specialist had just walked out of the room and Molly held the once-dreaded forms in her hand. A copy of her medical board. Nothing had changed.

She'd already met with the registered dietitian down the hall for an assessment and had discussed setting up a meal plan, but even following the most stringent of diets wouldn't affect the final recommendation. She would never get to fly again. Molly could try to appeal, but realistically, there was no chance it would be overturned as long as she required insulin. The process would take months and meant she'd be assigned as a "random tasker," riding a desk or shuffling files or whatever job the Air Force could find for her while she waited for them to ultimately reject her anyway.

She was done fighting. She was done pretending that she could keep doing what she'd always done. Yet, she wasn't angry or sad or grieving. In fact, Molly was surprisingly calm. Or, at least, way more calm than she'd expected. The decision had been taken out of her hands and she would be a good airman and follow orders.

It was time to move on.

She got dressed and threw the forms in her tote bag. The sun warmed her face the second she stepped into the parking lot. She had her whole future in front of her and suddenly it didn't look so dark. Sure, she had no idea what she would do or how she would do it. But she also didn't feel so alone anymore.

Maxine had wanted to come to the appointment with her, but Molly didn't want anyone influencing her decision. While it was a relief that everything was now out in the open, she wasn't totally willing to give up her independence. Knowing that she had her sister's full support in whatever she decided was reassuring enough.

Steering onto the highway, Molly determined that the first order of business for her new civilian life would be to get rid of the rental car and invest in something more permanent. And definitely more fast. If she couldn't be inside a jet, she would need to get her speed from somewhere else.

Her second order of business would be to find a job. Even if it was only temporary. Maxine had offered to put her to work at the bakery, but while she'd grown attached to the cute little shops and the people of Sugar Falls, Molly was holding out for a position that would utilize her aeronautical engineering degree. Besides, working with cookies all day might not be the best place for her, given that she was still learning the maneuvers of her daily nutritional minefield.

There were plenty of civilian contractors who designed military-grade planes. Maybe she should interview with one of those firms. For the first time in over a month, Molly finally saw that the world was full of possibilities. If nothing else, she could thank Kaleb for coming up with the idea of staying in the same field.

She looked up in the sky, wondering if he'd already hopped aboard his corporate jet, eagerly returning to his own life. She'd checked her cell phone several times this morning, hoping he'd call or even send her a text to tell her goodbye. But after the very public fight they'd had yesterday, she couldn't really blame him for wanting nothing else to do with her. If what Maxine had said about him not wanting to let her go was true, the determined man would've reached out by now.

Okay, enough of that. She zeroed in on the pavement and yellow dotted lines ahead of her. Her third order of business would be to forget about Kaleb and the amazing week they'd spent together.

Unfortunately, that would've been way easier to do if she hadn't spotted his dad's truck pulled over alongside the highway, the back axis sitting at an odd angle. Molly slowed down as she approached, then waited until an SUV passed before flipping a U-turn and pulling up behind him.

He was sitting cross-legged on the asphalt beside the tire he'd just pulled off, black smudges on his fingers and a confused expression on his face.

"Car problems?" she asked as she slammed her door shut and walked toward him.

He startled at her approach, but he was so focused on his task he didn't stand up. "I hit something in the road and popped my tire. I'm trying to change it."

"Have you ever changed one by yourself?" She squatted down next to him.

"No. But as you can see, I'm more than halfway there."

"How long have you been here?"

"About an hour or so."

"And nobody stopped to help you?"

"Plenty of people did. But I waved them on."

She slipped her phone out of her pocket and saw a full signal of bars. So he clearly wasn't out of cell service. "Why didn't you just call someone?"

"Because I can do it myself."

"Where's your tablet?" she asked, scanning the area around him. "Surely you watched a how-to video…"

"Nope. I'm determined to do it on my own."

She nodded, then stood up and put her hands in her back pockets. "Then you might want to go grab that lug nut that rolled under that hedge over there."

He muttered an expletive before rising and stomping toward the bushes. "I probably would've solved that problem. Eventually."

"Yeah, I hear that attitude is going around lately." Molly picked up the spare and lined the rim up with the lug bolts. "Unless you want to be out here for another hour, pass me the wrench."

"Listen. I'm sorry for making you think that I didn't believe you could handle things on your own." He passed the lug nuts to her one at a time.

She sighed. "How could you when I didn't even believe in myself?"

"But you were right about me being a micromanager. I saw a problem and I wanted to fix it."

"You thought I was a problem that needed fixing?"

"No. I'm getting this all wrong. Let me try and explain." He adjusted his glasses, leaving a smear of grease on his nose. "When I was in ninth grade, I was recovering from my second back surgery. We were driving home from my doctor's appointment and swung by the batting cages to pick up my brothers. At an intersection, this minivan in front of us broke down and was blocking the lane. All of my brothers jumped out to help push the car to safety, but my mom reached over and grabbed ahold of my seat belt buckle, not letting me unclasp it so that I could get out and help, too. The woman in the other car was crying and thanking my brothers and came over to the window to tell my mother that her sons were heroes. I never got to be a hero. Then, when I saw you in the grocery store that day, it was finally my chance."

Molly used the crank to lower the jack and slide it out. She stood up and wiped her hands on her jeans. "So now we're even. You saved me back in Duncan's Market and now I'm the one saving you on the side of the road."

"That's the thing, though, Molly." He hefted the old tire into the back of the truck. "I initially thought I was rescuing you, but it turned out that you saved me in more ways than you could imagine."

Her heart spun like a propeller and her head began to buzz. "What do you mean?"

Kaleb turned to her. "I was so absorbed in my company, in my life back in Seattle, in all my electronic gadgets. But then you bumped into me and suddenly I had something else to focus on. Something that was real, that wasn't just a game or a way to improve profits. For the first time in a long time, I felt needed. I felt necessary."

Her throat tightened. She'd never been anyone's focus. All her life, she'd been flying under the radar, trying not to draw any attention to herself. How did she respond to this?

"I'm pretty sure that you were the one who bumped into me," she murmured, not knowing what else to say.

"And I'm pretty sure that even small-town grocery stores have video surveillance."

"Well, if anyone could get their hands on it, you could."

He winced. "Listen, I'm sorry about calling the Pentagon and all that overhanded business with your commanding officer. It was totally out of line. And I promise I'll never get involved in your life like that again."

The propeller feeling stopped and she gulped. The finality of his statement sounded more like a threat than a promise because it was coupled with the fact that he was leaving today. Of course he would never get involved in her life again because he had no future plans to ever be in it.

"So…" She handed him the wrench. "Were you on your way to Boise or did you arrange for your corporate jet to meet you at a local airfield?"

His eyes did a double blink behind his glasses. "No, I was on my way to Shadowview but my watch battery died and my alarm didn't go off. I guess I missed your doctor's appointment?"

"Wait. You were driving to see *me*? At the hospital?"

"That's where you were, right?"

"Yes. But what I mean is, why?"

"To apologize. And, you know, to provide some moral support when you got the lab reports."

"But you just said you weren't going to interfere in my life again?"

"I meant like a boss."

"Is there a different way for how you do things?"

"Not really. But if we're going to be together, you might have to indulge me sometimes."

"Be together? Like as a couple?"

"Look, I know you said that you weren't ready for a relationship and needed some time to figure your life out. I have no problem with that and am more than happy to wait."

She put her hands on her hips. "Kaleb Chatterson,

have you ever had to wait for anything in your entire life?"

He looked to the side as if he was doing some quick calculations. "Not really. But I've waited twenty-eight years for you already, so I figure what's a couple more weeks?"

"A couple more weeks? You're pretty confident of yourself."

"Nah. I'm just confidant that you'll come to the right conclusion," he said, putting his hands on her waist and drawing her closer. "Eventually."

She wiped the grease off his nose. "And what conclusion is that?"

"That I love you." His lips brushed across hers and she lost her breath. "That I need you." His second kiss lasted a split second longer and she became light-headed. "That I can build you your very own flight simulator."

She wrapped her arms around his neck, joy ricocheting inside her. "Maybe I don't need a few weeks, after all."

"Was it the flight simulator that convinced you?" Kaleb nuzzled her neck.

"That was part of it." She smiled.

"What was the other?"

"The promise of another family vacation with all the Chattersons?"

He groaned and squeezed her tighter.

She giggled. "Okay, I give up. The other part is that I love you, too, Kaleb."

"Yeah?" He tapped the screen on his watch. "Say it again so I can record it."

She brought his hand back down to her waist. "I

love you. I didn't realize it until last night when my sister came to check on me and I was so disappointed it wasn't you."

"I was going to run after you, but my dad told me I should let you cool off. And he was worried I'd get pneumonia and my mom would blame him."

She cringed. "Sorry for sending you into the dunk tank."

"You have a pretty good arm, but I deserved it. I never should have interfered with your life like that. You trusted me with something huge and I tried to use it to my advantage."

"I never should have made you keep my condition a secret in the first place. When the military placed me on leave, I had never been so lost and so afraid. I thought my condition was bigger than me, and as much as I needed to control it, I couldn't. I'd always been able to do things on my own and then, in a matter of weeks, I felt all alone. But then I came to Sugar Falls and it's quite impossible to ever feel alone here. Like seriously. Nobody would leave me alone. And I needed that. I needed you to show me that it was okay to allow myself to be vulnerable, to let someone else look after me. I needed my sister and Kylie and Julia and all the other ladies in town to show me that it was okay to share, to be myself. I'm not saying that I'm glad I have diabetes or that things are going to be easy from here on out. But now that everything is out in the open, I'm finally seeing how strong I can be."

"Just know that you don't always have to be strong." He pulled her closer. "I'll love you whether you're having a bad day or a good one."

She stood on her tiptoes, pressed her lips to his and showed him just how great of a day she planned to have.

## *Epilogue*

*Seattle, four months later...*

"Did I really need to put on my old flight suit for this, Kaleb?" Molly asked, her voice echoing inside a cavernous room on the ground floor of Perfect Game Industries.

"I wanted everything to be authentic," Kaleb replied, his hand still covering her eyes.

"Can I look yet?"

"Almost." He positioned her a few inches to the left. "I feel like we need Hunter here to do his knife and fork drumroll on the table."

"Kaleb!"

"Okay. One. Two. Three. Open."

Molly's eyes widened and her mouth formed an O. "Whoa!"

"Well, what do you think?" Kaleb asked, a proud grin stretching across his face.

"When you said you were going to make a flight simulator, I thought you meant like one of those faux cockpits you sit in at the arcade. I didn't think you meant an actual, full-scale model of an FA-18 Hornet."

The replica jet sat on some sort of raised mechanism that housed all the components for a moving simulator. A huge movie screen lined the wall in front.

"Well, this is a one-of-a-kind prototype. The final models will be a third of this size because they'll be cheaper to ship and won't take up as much room in the VA rehab hospitals."

"Still, how were you able to make this look so realistic?"

Kaleb cleared his throat. "You know my contact at the Pentagon? Well, he talked to the people over at McDonnell Douglas and they sold me the prefabricated pieces—at double the government cost, I might add. Plus, I had to get top secret clearance and sign these papers promising I'd never sell it to our enemies."

"This is amazing. Looks like you didn't need to hire me as a consultant, after all." Molly had been traveling with Kaleb to various air and space museums around the country—the pilot of the corporate jet always letting her ride up front with him when she wanted—so they could do research while she waited for her discharge paperwork to come in. She would've thought that being around all the planes might depress her, but it ended up motivating her to go back to school and get her graduate degree in aeronautical design. She'd moved into Kaleb's apartment two months ago and registered for classes at the University of Washington.

"Oh, don't worry. You're going to earn your paycheck. I need you to climb inside and tell me if the motion part is realistic. But I'm forewarning you, we have a lot of bugs to work out still."

He followed her as she scrambled up the steel caged steps to the cockpit. She used the outside crank to open the dome-shaped canopy. She was about to climb inside when he said, "Wait!"

He pulled off a piece of tan paper taped to the side of the aircraft to reveal the stenciled letters.

CAPT MOLLY MARKHAM

Her hand flew to her mouth. "You mean it's mine? You built me my own jet?"

He shrugged as if all he'd done was given her a gift card to the Cowgirl Up Café. "I didn't want you to miss out on your old life."

"Kaleb, you are the most incredible man I've ever met."

"Keep that in mind when you see the next part."

"What next part?" she asked, and he motioned to another rectangle of tan paper after her name.

She peeled it back to see a hyphen and an additional name. It took her a second to put it together and when she did she gasped.

CAPT MOLLY MARKHAM-CHATTERSON

"Does this mean…" she started to say as she turned to look at him. Tears filled her eyes when she realized he was down on one knee, holding open a jewelry box with a… "Um, is that a smartwatch?"

Kaleb looked down.

"Hold on," he said as he tapped on the screen. When it lit up, a picture of a diamond solitaire blinked back at her.

Molly tilted her head to the side. "Are you proposing to me with a digital ring?"

"The real one is hidden inside your flight suit," he said, reaching for the zipper at her neck. "If you agree to marry me, I'll help you find it."

Molly's heart spun into a nosedive and all she could do was tearfully nod yes, then happily, actively, help him search.

\* \* \* \* \*

*Don't miss Christy Jeffries's next book*
*THE MAVERICK'S BRIDAL BARGAIN*
*Available June 2018!*

*And for more* AMERICAN HEROES *stories,*
*check out these books:*
*CLAIMING THE CAPTAIN'S BABY*
*by Rochelle Alers*
*A SOLDIER IN CONARD COUNTY*
*by Rachel Lee*
*Available now!*

*And in April, look for*
*SOLDIER, HANDYMAN, FAMILY MAN*
*by Lynne Marshall*

*Available wherever Harlequin Special Edition*
*books and ebooks are sold.*

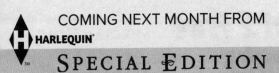

# COMING NEXT MONTH FROM

# HARLEQUIN®

# SPECIAL EDITION

## Available March 20, 2018

### #2611 FORTUNE'S FAMILY SECRETS
*The Fortunes of Texas: The Rulebreakers* • by Karen Rose Smith
Nash Fortune Tremont is an undercover detective staying at the Bluebonnet
Bed and Breakfast. Little does he know, the woman he's been spilling his
secrets to has some of her own. When Cassie's secrets come to light, will their
budding relationship survive the lies?

### #2612 HER MAN ON THREE RIVERS RANCH
*Men of the West* • by Stella Bagwell
When widow Katherine O'Dell literally runs into rancher Blake Hollister on
the sidewalk, she's not looking for love. She and her son have already come
second to a man's career, but Blake is determined to make them his family
and prove to Katherine that she'll always be first in his heart.

### #2613 THE BABY SWITCH!
*The Wyoming Multiples* • by Melissa Senate
When Liam Mercer, a wealthy single father, and Shelby Ingalls, a struggling
single mother, discover their babies were switched at birth, they marry for
convenience...and unexpectedly fall in love!

### #2614 A KISS, A DANCE & A DIAMOND
*The Cedar River Cowboys* • by Helen Lacey
Fifteen years ago, Kieran O'Sullivan shattered Nicola Radici's heart and left
town. Now he's back—and if her nephews have their way, wedding bells
might be in their future!

### #2615 FROM BEST FRIEND TO DADDY
*Return to Stonerock* • by Jules Bennett
After one night of passion leads to pregnancy, best friends Kate McCoy and
Gray Gallagher have to navigate their new relationship and the fact that they
each want completely different—and conflicting—things out of life.

### #2616 SOLDIER, HANDYMAN, FAMILY MAN
*American Heroes* • by Lynne Marshall
Mark Delaney has been drifting since returning home from the army. When
he meets Laurel Prescott, a widow with three children who's faced struggles
of her own, he thinks he might have just found the perfect person to make a
fresh start with.

---

**YOU CAN FIND MORE INFORMATION ON UPCOMING HARLEQUIN® TITLES,
FREE EXCERPTS AND MORE AT WWW.HARLEQUIN.COM.**

HSECNM0318

# Get 2 Free Books,

## Plus 2 Free Gifts—

just for trying the
## Reader Service!

"Are you going to switch the babies back?"

Shelby froze.

Liam felt momentarily sick.

It was the first time anyone had actually asked that question.

"No, ma'am," Liam said. "I have a better idea."

Shelby glanced at him, questions in her eyes.

"Where is my soup!" Kate's mother called again.

"You go ahead, Kate," Shelby said, stepping out onto the porch. "Thanks for talking to us."

Kate nodded and shut the door behind them.

Liam leaned his head back and he started down the porch steps. "I need about ten cups of coffee or a bottle of scotch."

"I thought I might fall over when she asked about switching the babies back," Shelby said, her face pale, her green eyes troubled. She stared at him. "You said you had a better idea. What is it? I sure need to hear it. Because switching the babies is not an option. Right?"

"Damned straight it's not. Never will be. Shane is your son. Alexander is my son. No matter what. Alexander will also become your son and Shane will also become my son as the days pass and all this sinks in."

"I think so, too," she said. "Right now it's like we can't even process that babies we didn't know until Friday are ours biologically. But as we begin to accept it, I'll start to feel a connection to Alexander. Same with you and Shane."

He nodded. "Exactly. Which is why on the way here, I started thinking about a way to ease us into that, to give us both what we need and want."

She tilted her head, waiting.

He thought he had the perfect solution. The only solution.

"I called the lab running the DNA tests and threw a bucket of money at them to expedite the results. On Monday," he continued, "we will officially know for absolute certain that our babies were switched. Of course we're not going to switch them back. I'd sooner cut off my arm."

"Me, too," Shelby said, staring at him. "So what's your plan?"

"The plan is for us to get married."

Shelby's mouth dropped open. "What? We've been living together for a day. Now we're getting married. Legally wed? Till death do us part?"

*Don't miss*
*THE BABY SWITCH! by Melissa Senate,*
*available April 2018 wherever*
*Harlequin® Special Edition books and ebooks are sold.*

www.Harlequin.com

*LOVE*
# Harlequin
# romance?

Join our Harlequin community to share your thoughts and connect with other romance readers!

Be the first to find out about promotions, news, and exclusive content!

Sign up for the Harlequin e-newsletter and download a free book from any series at

## www.TryHarlequin.com

---

**CONNECT WITH US AT:**

Harlequin.com/Community

 Facebook.com/HarlequinBooks

 Twitter.com/HarlequinBooks

 Instagram.com/HarlequinBooks

 Pinterest.com/HarlequinBooks

ReaderService.com

**ROMANCE WHEN
YOU NEED IT**

HSOCIAL2017

# THE WORLD IS BETTER WITH

## *Romance*

Harlequin has everything from contemporary, passionate and heartwarming to suspenseful and inspirational stories.

Whatever your mood, we have a romance just for you!

Connect with us to find your next great read, special offers and more.

f /HarlequinBooks

@HarlequinBooks

www.HarlequinBlog.com

www.Harlequin.com/Newsletters